Wild Winter

Samantha Baca

Contents

One
Georgia

"Are you sure it's going to fit?" I asked, stepping back to look as my husband and his best friend, Dex, tried to shove the small twin-size mattress through the narrow space to get it lined up on the frame.

"We'll make it," Alex grunted as he pushed harder, showing off the defined muscles I admired on my husband.

"I really don't mind sleeping on the couch," Dex said as they maneuvered in the small space.

"Fuck that. You came to help us. The least I can do is give you a proper place to sleep. I just wish my grandma would have told me we wouldn't have heat up here. Could have saved this trip for the summer instead of trying to get things done during a fucking blizzard."

"It's not a problem. I don't mind helping," Dex replied as they dropped the mattress onto the frame and stared at it.

When Alex's grandma had called and asked if he could help with a few repairs at the cabin, she failed to mention just how many there were. Not only was the heater not working, but the guest bathroom was out of order due to plumbing issues. The kitchen had started to be remodeled, but the work was never finished. Then there was a giant hole in the wall in the living room with no explanation as to why. This left us with three people needing to share the only functional bedroom and bathroom.

"I saw some wood gathered by the back door. I'll get a fire started, and then we can settle in for the night. Sorry about the cramped space," Alex said, shoving a hand through his short hair.

I chewed my lip as I looked around the room and saw how we would literally be on top of each other. There was nothing separating the two beds, except for a small gap between the mattresses, making it one large bed that I would share with my husband and his best friend.

I swallowed hard, ignoring the curious glance from my husband as heat spread across my neck and up my face while I forced the inappropriate thoughts out of my head. His lips curled into a slight smirk as if he knew exactly what I was thinking. I looked away and tucked a strand of hair behind my ear, avoiding his gaze.

"I don't need much," Dex replied with a shrug as he shoved his hands into his jeans and smiled.

I could already feel the tension in the air as they both studied me.

It didn't take much for them to notice something was going on. Between the flushed skin and the change in my breathing, I had everyone's attention. But that was the thing about being so close to Dex, he could read me as well as my husband. There were no secrets between the three of us other than the dark desires I had been harboring since the day I first met them back in college. While I had immediately fallen for Alex, I could never deny the attraction I felt for Dex.

"Everything alright?" Alex asked, stepping in front of me and lifting my chin between his fingers as he forced me to look at him.

"Yeah. Why?" I responded a little too breathlessly.

He chuckled softly and arched an eyebrow as he called me on my bullshit.

"Just checking. You seem a little *flustered*."

I rubbed my lips together and looked past him to find Dex fighting a grin as he stared down at the bed and ran a finger along the scruff on his jaw.

"Nope. Just cold. And tired," I lied, rocking back on my heels as I pretended to shiver.

I was far from cold. The room could be covered in ice, and I would easily set it on fire with the heat radiating through me at the thought of sharing a bed with both of them tonight. What made it even worse was that Alex was well aware of how easily I was turned on by the thought of being with two men. We had talked about it several times, and it had been discussed in filthy detail, quickly bringing me to orgasm every single time. The only thing that *hadn't* been discussed was how often I imagined his best friend as the man who joined us.

"Oh. Good. Because I would hate to make things *hard* for you," Alex replied, chewing his lower lip as Dex turned and coughed to hide the laugh that spilled out of him. I had no idea if Alex ever talked to Dex about our sex life. I couldn't imagine he would, but then again, they were best friends, and there wasn't much they didn't talk about.

"You're the worst," I hissed, leaning up on my tiptoes to reach his ears so Dex couldn't hear me. I shook my head and went to pull away when his arm snaked around my waist. He pulled me against his chest, pinning me with a look that was anything but playful.

"No, baby. I'm the best, and you know it. Why don't you go take a shower, and I'll help you relax before bed."

My eyebrows rose as I stared at him in disbelief. Was he kidding me right now? Dex was standing *right* there! The last thing I was going to do was allow my husband to make me come when his best friend was less than a few feet away, even if it was one of my fantasies. But that was the problem—this was real life, not a fantasy.

"But—" I started before he pressed a finger over my lips to stop me.

"I'm not going to fight with you on this, Georgia. Go take a shower. You know you always feel better after a long, hot one."

I knew my face gave away what I was thinking when he chuckled again and shook his head.

I pulled a deep breath in and let it out slowly as I turned on my heel and grabbed the duffel bag I had packed for what was supposed to be a two-night stay at the cabin. Thanks to the blizzard raging outside, I wouldn't be surprised if we got stuck even longer.

I entered the small bathroom attached to the bedroom and closed the door behind me. My face was still flushed, and

I knew it was going to be a very long night trying to avoid the feelings stirring deep inside of me.

Two
Alex

"I can sleep in the living room," Dex offered after we heard the shower turn on in the bathroom.

I grabbed the clean sheets and tossed a set to Dex for his bed. The beds were already stripped when we arrived, and all the linens needed to be washed. My grandma was in the process of moving into an assisted living facility and wanted to sell the cabin since she was no longer able to visit and enjoy it. Unfortunately, there was a lot that needed to be done before it would be ready to list, so I offered to come up for the weekend and help with the repairs. Georgia had recommended bringing our own linens, which was a good call given the quilts my grandma had were from the seventies. It had been years since anyone had used the cabin, and the deterioration was starting to show.

"I'm not going to have you sleep in the living room. It's freezing in there."

The fireplace in the bedroom crackled as I stepped around the front of the bed. I had made sure to start it right away so Georgia wouldn't be cold after she got out of the shower. I waited for Dex to move his mattress slightly so I could lift mine to pull the fitted sheet over the queen-sized mattress Georgia and I would be sleeping on. It was smaller than the king-sized bed we had at home, but we would make it work. Besides, it was freezing balls in here, so we had a good excuse to cuddle and share body heat.

"I don't want to make Georgia uncomfortable sleeping in here," Dex said as he tossed the flat sheet onto the bed and stared at me.

"You're not," I assured him, turning my attention to the pillows we had brought with us. Georgia really had thought of everything, which made me feel like shit for teasing her about bringing so much when we were only staying for a few nights. With the storm raging outside, we would be here even longer than that.

"You're so full of shit. I know most of Georgia's looks, but that one was new. I would never do anything to make her uneasy, so if I need to sleep in another room, I will."

I turned and looked at him, wondering how to tell him what the problem was without embarrassing my wife. Being married to her for over ten years meant that we didn't keep stuff from each other, including her fantasies about being with two men at the same time. We'd talked about those fantasies a time or two during sex when we would picture adding someone else, but now that she was literally going to be sleeping between two guys, I could imagine how wild her imagination was running. Even though there were technically two beds, neither of them was big enough to give the three of us that much space without being on top of each other. My cock twitched at the thought of what Georgia might be doing in the shower to relieve some of the tension she no doubt had been feeling.

"Trust me. She's fine. She'll be better after her shower."

I would make sure she was. Even if I had to sneak around my best friend and take care of my wife while he was sleeping a few feet away, I would make sure Georgia was taken care of. Nothing gave me greater joy than bringing her to climax and feeling her body respond to my touch.

"I was thinking about starting on the guest bathroom tomorrow," I said, changing the subject before Georgia finished in the shower.

"That works for me. We can take a look in the morning and see what we need. You said there's a store close by?"

"Yeah, about twenty minutes away. There's not much up here, but at least we can get basic supplies and stock up on food while we're here."

We had packed a few ice chests full of stuff for what we thought would be a few days up here, but now that I knew how bad the storm was, there was no doubt we would need to get more supplies.

"Cool. We can make a list, and then I can run out to get stuff."

I loved that even though we were technically secluded on the top of the mountain, there was a whole little community up here, so we didn't have to figure out how to get back down the mountain to get what we needed. There was the general store that had almost everything you could think of, a gas station, and a single restaurant that served breakfast, lunch, and dinner.

I sat down on the bed and grabbed the remote for the TV that was mounted above the dresser. It was getting late, and there was a full day's work ahead of us tomorrow if I wanted to make progress and get everything done on time.

The shower turned off, and I waited patiently for Georgia to come out while Dex lay on the other bed and played on his phone.

The bathroom door squeaked open—another thing I would need to fix—and Georgia's head poked out.

"Can you come help me?" she asked, holding the door as closed as possible.

I glanced at Dex, noticing the way he purposely avoided looking at her. He must have heard the same worry in her voice that I did. I should have thought to thoroughly check the bathroom before she took a shower since I knew how common it was to find critters in the cabin, especially when it had been a while since anyone had been there.

"Hey, baby. What's wrong?" I asked, standing in front of the door as she slowly stepped back to let me in.

Warm fog wrapped around me as my eyes traveled down the length of her body. I opened my mouth to ask her what was wrong but closed it when it clicked.

"I didn't know we would be sharing a room," she said quietly, tugging at the bottom of her see-through t-shirt that she usually wore to bed.

"It's okay. Did you bring anything else you can sleep in for tonight?"

She looked over at the duffel bag that was open on the counter by the sink. Peeking out of the top were bits of red and black lace.

"I thought I would surprise you with new lingerie this weekend," she whispered, lowering her head as she tugged at her shirt again.

"Fuck," I groaned, tossing my head back as my cock hardened.

"I know. I'm sorry. I don't know what else to do. I brought jeans and bulky sweaters—neither of which is comfortable to sleep in."

"I meant *fuck* because I can just imagine how fucking sexy those are going to look on you, and now I can't stop thinking about it," I clarified as I ran a hand down my face in frustration.

"Can you focus on the real problem here?"

"Trust me—I am," I growled as I took her hand and ran it over the thick bulge pressing against my joggers.

"Alex!" she squealed, looking past me to where the door was cracked open.

"What? You can't expect that I won't get hard thinking about you naked or wearing lingerie, Georgia. All you have to do is breathe and I'm hard."

"Okay, first of all—you're being ridiculous. Second, what are we going to do about this?" she hissed as she pointed to her t-shirt.

"Give me a minute." I turned and walked out of the bathroom, closing the door behind me.

Dex looked up from his phone with his eyebrows raised in silent question.

"Do you have a t-shirt Georgia can borrow? My bag is still in the truck, and I don't want to go out in the snow to try to get it."

"Yeah. Help yourself. My bag is in the living room."

I nodded and left the room, turning on the lights so I didn't trip over anything. I grabbed his bag and pulled out the first T-shirt I found.

"Here you go," I said as I handed it to Georgia after slipping back into the bathroom.

She smiled and took it after pulling her shirt over her head and tossing it on the counter. I groaned and bit my lip as her perky tits greeted me, nipples fully hard and begging to be sucked. She pulled the new shirt over her head and looked in the mirror.

"I should have brought shorts to sleep in," she said, still studying her reflection as she tugged at the bottom of it.

"It's fine. The shirt is long enough to cover you."

"Where did you get this? I don't think I've seen it on—" She stopped as she looked down at the image on the front of it, and her eyes widened. "Why am I wearing Dex's shirt?"

"Because my bag is still in the truck, and his was in the living room."

"Alex," she whined, closing her eyes as her head fell forward.

"What? What's the problem?"

"The problem is that I'm wearing your best friend's t-shirt to bed with nothing else on."

"So?"

"So, I think it's a little inappropriate that his shirt is covering my bare breasts. That when he goes to wear it, it's going to smell like me," she replied as she lifted the fabric and pulled it to her nose. "Or that *I'm* going to smell like *him*."

"I think you're overthinking all of this, baby. It's just a shirt. Let's head to bed, and then we can get you some clothes to sleep in tomorrow."

She scrunched her face and kept staring down at the shirt as I stood behind her and wrapped my arms around her waist.

"Fine, but when I smell like another man, you can't be mad at me."

I caught her eye in the mirror and held her gaze.

"You could smell like Dex anytime, and I would never be mad. He's my best friend, Georgia."

A rush of color flushed her face as she chewed her lower lip. I knew I was planting the wrong ideas in her head, yet I couldn't bring myself to stop.

Three
Georgia

"Right there," I whimpered as Dex slid his tongue along my slit and stopped at my clit. He sucked hard, pulling it between his lips as I dug my nails into the sheets.

My nipples were hard as I brushed my hands over them, needing the extra stimulation to take my mind off how amazing it felt to have Dex eating my pussy.

"That's it, baby," Alex coaxed, sitting in a chair across from us, watching as he stroked his cock.

I turned my head and watched, loving how he took his time caressing his shaft. I licked my lips, wanting to suck it while Dex tortured my pussy. As if reading my mind, Alex got up and crossed the room until he was standing beside the bed, close enough for me to reach him.

I propped myself up on my elbows the best I could and wrapped my hand around his cock. My tongue teased the tip, making him hiss as Dex sucked my clit harder before inserting a finger inside of me.

I gasped at the contact as my pussy gripped him tighter, wanting him to fuck me already.

"It's so fucking hot to see Dex eating your pussy," Alex said as his eyes focused on his best friend's head between my legs.

"She tastes amazing," Dex said, pulling away slightly as he changed position and started stimulating my G-spot with his fingers. I moaned and closed my eyes as I enjoyed the sensation while taking Alex's cock to the back of my throat.

"Should I make her squirt?" Dex asked, not to me but to my husband, who got harder in my mouth at the thought.

"Fuck, yeah. Make her squirt," Alex replied.

I moaned louder, arching my back as Dex began putting pressure where I needed it as he lowered his mouth and sucked my clit again. I knew I couldn't focus on giving Alex a proper blow job while Dex was about to send me over the edge. I loosened my jaw and opened as wide as I could as he slid in deeper, touching the back of my throat. I opened my eyes and nodded, letting him know he could fuck my mouth.

His hand gripped the back of my head, holding me in place as he thrust hard, triggering my gag reflex. I whimpered as he did it again, this time getting even deeper.

"You're perfection, Georgia," Alex said from above me, continuing to fuck my mouth the way I wanted him to.

Before I could try to respond with his thick cock in my mouth, I felt the first wave of pleasure wash over me as Dex made me come. My pussy trembled with need as fluid rushed out of me. I moaned louder, pure ecstasy taking over me.

"Baby, wake up," Alex whispered, gently kissing my shoulder as he pulled me against his chest.

My eyes fluttered open, a few seconds passing as I took in my surroundings to figure out where I was. I noticed Dex sleeping beside me first. Had he always been that close to me? If I moved even an inch, I would be pressed against his body. The light scent of his cologne filled the space around us, making my body hum with desire.

I looked over my shoulder and found my husband's heated gaze on my face.

"Let me take care of you," he said softly, pulling me back to the other side of the bed.

"I'm fine," I replied quietly to keep from waking Dex.

I knew my face was still flushed from the dream I'd just had, and if he touched my panties, he would feel just how wet they were.

"No, you're not. You need a release," he countered as he kissed the side of my neck.

He was curled behind me as we both lay on our sides facing Dex.

"How do you know?" I asked, my eyes fluttering closed as his mouth moved down my shoulder while his hand slid across my stomach and pulled Dex's t-shirt up.

"You were moaning in your sleep."

A wave of embarrassment washed over me, but I couldn't focus on it with his hand slipping under my panties.

"Fuck, Georgia," he moaned quietly as his finger slid through the wetness as he parted me. "You're fucking drenched, and your clit is so swollen. You need to come, baby. Let me take care of this for you."

"But Dex is right there," I whispered.

"Then you'll just have to be quiet," he warned, leaning up to nip my ear as he slid another finger inside of me.

My back arched as I leaned into him, spreading my legs to allow him full access. It wouldn't take much for him to get me off, given how ready I was for him already, but my mind wouldn't shut up about how close Dex was to us. As if sensing my unease, he slowly pulled his fingers out, kissed me gently on the lips, then lowered himself under the covers until his face was lined up with my pussy.

I tried to regulate my breathing as I felt him push my lace panties to the side before his lips trailed over my slit, licking every ounce of wetness up. His tongue flicked rapidly against my clit, driving me wild as my back arched, and I tried to stifle the moan that wanted to come out.

My lips pressed together as he grabbed my hips and held me in place while he ate my pussy. It was as good—if not better—than what Dex did in my dream. Not that he wasn't doing a good job in my dream, but real life was always better, and my husband was determined to make me come.

I reached down and gripped his head, holding him in place as the first waves of pleasure washed over me. My head fell to the side as my pussy continued to spasm. I opened my eyes and found Dex on his side, watching me.

His eyes stayed locked on mine as the pleasure took hold of me, sending me over the edge with each spasm. It wasn't until I was done and trying to regulate my breathing that he rolled on his back and closed his eyes as if he hadn't just watched me come from his best friend eating my pussy.

Four
Alex

"Dex saw you last night," Georgia hissed at me as I stood at the coffee pot, trying to figure out how the thing worked.

"What are you talking about?" I asked, a little distracted without my daily caffeine to get my day started.

Georgia reached over and smacked my hand, bringing my focus to her. She raised her eyebrows, and it immediately clicked. She was talking about last night when I went down on her to relieve her tension.

"Are you sure?"

"Yes! I looked over, and he was looking right at me!" she exclaimed, throwing her hands in the air.

Last night had been a long night, with me being restless in general. It didn't help that I woke up with a raging boner after eating my wife out and hearing her sweet moans every time I drifted to sleep. I had wanted to do more but didn't want to risk getting caught by Dex. Too late for that, I guess.

"I'm sure everything is fine," I said, grabbing her by the waist and pulling her into me.

"He. Saw. You. Go. Down. On. Me. What's fine about that?"

I shrugged and felt a smirk playing at the corners of my lips.

Her eyes widened as she smacked my chest with her hand.

"Alex! I'm being serious. We need to talk about this before he gets out of the shower."

"What is there to talk about? I ate my wife's pussy last night after she woke me up while having a very erotic dream. It's not like we committed a crime or something."

"No, but you performed a *sexual* act on your wife with your best friend literally a few feet away."

I pressed my lips together and scrunched my face.

"What is that look for?" she asked, moving her pointer finger in a circle in the general direction of my face. "What aren't you telling me?"

"Nothing. I swear."

"Don't you fucking lie to me," she warned, playfully shoving me.

Georgia was downright gorgeous, but she was so fucking cute when she was angry that sometimes I liked to press her buttons just to get her riled up. Not only that, but it made for incredible make-up sex.

"It's not like it would be the first time it's happened," I answered, grinning when I saw her face change as she processed what that meant.

"You've gone down on a girl with Dex right beside you before?" she asked in a hushed tone.

The water was still running, which was our sign that Dex was still in the shower.

"A couple of times."

"Alex!"

"What?" I shrugged again as a laugh bubbled up. "People do crazy shit in college."

"*We* met in college. So was all of this crazy shit while you were with me?"

"Fuck no. You do remember that I am two years older than you, right?"

She nodded, still eyeing me suspiciously.

"Yes…"

"So that means I had two years in college before we met. A lot happened in those two years, Georgia."

She shook her head as if clearing the thoughts that were flooding it.

"Why didn't you ever tell me this?"

"I don't know. I guess it never came up."

"We've talked about my *stuff*," she said, raising her eyebrows again. I loved how she was too shy to say what she really meant.

"Yes, but while your stuff was incredibly hot and a huge turn-on, it didn't involve anyone specifically. Meanwhile, my stuff directly involved someone you know. I don't think Dex would want me sharing stories about our wild days."

Her face immediately flushed crimson as she tried to turn away before I could see it.

"Nope, I don't think so," I said as I grabbed her and spun her back to face me. She looked everywhere but at me as the blush continued to cover her chest and neck.

"Who is it that you think about when you have those fantasies about two guys, Georgia?" I asked, knowing that if I pushed too hard, she wasn't going to tell me.

"No one," she lied, her voice rising an octave to give her away.

"Georgia," I warned, leaning in front of her to keep her from looking past me.

She chewed her lower lip as she avoided my eyes.

"Your fantasies are about Dex," I said, surprising myself as the words tumbled out.

Her head whipped up as she stared at me, a mixture of fear and embarrassment playing on her face. She pushed away from me, but I was too stunned by my realization to keep my hold on her.

"You want to fuck my best friend."

I crossed my arms over my chest and looked at my beautiful wife. While I had considered a time or two that she might have been thinking of Dex when she talked about her fantasy of being with two guys at the same time, I never imagined it would be true.

I licked my lips and debated how to proceed when the sound of the shower shut off. Georgia turned and walked away, but this time, I didn't stop her. Both of us needed some time to think about what happened last night and what it meant for our marriage.

26

<u>Five</u>
Georgia

"You sure you don't want to go with us?" Alex asked as Dex pulled on his coat and fixed the beanie on his head.

"Yeah. I'm fine staying here. You said it would be a quick trip to the store anyway," I replied, hoping my husband wouldn't question why I didn't want to be around them right now.

Last night had messed with my head between the inappropriate dream about Dex and then him actually watching me have an orgasm. Not only that, but now my husband knew that I had fantasies involving his best friend. I knew that eventually Alex and I would have to talk about that, but right now I just needed a few minutes alone to process my thoughts.

"Want us to bring anything back for you?" Dex offered, standing by the door as he looked me in the eyes.

My skin flushed seven shades of red as a vivid memory of last night popped up.

"Wine," I blurted out while nodding my head. If I were going to survive the weekend up here alone with them, I was going to need reinforcements.

I had taken a long shower while the guys started looking at what they needed for the repairs. It was so long that I didn't start shampooing my hair until the water was ice cold, and I had to shiver through the rest of it. Whatever hair I'd managed to shave from my legs had likely already grown back from the endless goosebumps I'd had since then. Not only that, but it was freaking cold in the kitchen, where we were all hanging out while the guys finished the list of things they needed from the store.

"Got it," Alex said, leaning in to kiss my forehead. "If you think of anything else, give me a call."

"I will. Love you."

"Love you too."

They turned to leave, and I noticed the faint smile on Dex's lips before he turned and followed behind Alex, pulling the door shut.

I shivered against the cold as I got up and went back to the bedroom. It was the warmest room in the house, which meant I had a good excuse to climb into bed and binge-watch TV until they got back.

****

I hadn't intended to fall asleep but woke up to the sound of the guys talking in the living room. I rubbed my eyes, thankful that I didn't have makeup on, then swung my legs over the side of the bed. Sitting on the nightstand beside me was a Twix candy bar. I smiled, knowing it was from Alex since he always liked to bring me a surprise whenever he went to the store.

I took it with me and grinned when I found the boys sitting at the small, rickety table in the kitchen. There was sandwich stuff on the counter, which was likely left out in case they wanted another sandwich.

"Hey, baby," Alex said around a mouthful of food. "Want me to make you a sandwich?"

I glanced at Dex right as he lifted his sandwich to his mouth and took a bite. I couldn't help but notice the way his full lips closed down on the bread and how his tongue swiped the crumbs away before he started chewing. It shouldn't have looked so erotic, but it did.

"I'm not very hungry, but thank you," I lied. "And thank you for the surprise treat." I held the Twix up and smiled.

"That was Dex's idea," Alex said, nodding his head toward him.

My expression changed from happy to confused in a matter of seconds.

Dex used his fingers to wipe the corners of his mouth, never breaking eye contact with me. He licked his lips, and my eyes immediately went to his mouth. I wondered what he could do with those plump lips or how good they would feel on my skin.

"I thought you could use a treat," Dex said, keeping his focus on me. "You seemed a little off this morning, and I wanted to make sure you were okay."

What he meant was: *I watched you come last night and felt bad about invading your privacy, so I bought you your favorite candy bar to say sorry.*

I nodded and rubbed my lips together, not trusting that I could say anything that wouldn't embarrass me.

I turned my focus to the counter and noticed several bottles of wine along with two bottles of whiskey.

"I really only needed one bottle," I said, hoping my tone came out as playful as I intended.

"Well, we grabbed a few extra since we got some bad news while we were at the store," Alex said, wincing as he looked at me.

"What's the bad news?"

"I think the question should be, what's the *good* news?" Dex teased, earning a fake glare from Alex.

"Well, for starters, the general store was very limited and didn't have the majority of the things we needed to do the repairs," Alex said, eyeing me carefully.

"Okay, what's the other bad news?"

"The blizzard that we drove in on our way up here was just the start of the storm. Apparently, there's another storm moving in, and we'll likely be stuck up here for a few weeks."

"A few weeks?!" My eyebrows shot up to my hairline as I stared at him in disbelief.

He nodded and got up, coming to stand in front of me.

"We'll have everything we need to get through the storm," he assured me. "Dex and I stocked up on food and bottled water while we were there. We also grabbed plenty of batteries and a few flashlights for when we lose power. Once I'm done eating, I'm going to go out to the shop in the back and cut some more firewood. I know it's not ideal, but it'll be okay."

"Alex, it's four weeks until Christmas, and you're telling me that we're stranded in this dilapidated cabin that has no heat except in the tiny bedroom we have to share," I nearly shouted, squeezing the Twix in my hand. I didn't want to hurt the candy bar because I was definitely going to need it later. I set it on the counter and tried to take a deep breath to calm myself, but failed.

We had decided to come up on the long weekend after Thanksgiving, hoping it would be enough time to get stuff fixed, but we never talked about the possibility of us getting stuck up here.

"I'm sorry, baby. There's nothing we can do. Even if we tried to get back down the mountain, it wouldn't be safe. They've closed the roads up here in anticipation of the storm. The general store is going to stay open as long as they can, but once they run out of supplies, they won't be able to get more until it's safe for them to open the road again."

"This is unbelievable," I groaned, letting my head fall forward as he pulled me against his chest and held me.

"It's not an ideal situation, but we'll make the best of it," he assured me.

<u>Six</u>

Dex

I tried to tune out the sound of the couple on the TV as they started going at it. It wasn't that it was weird watching a movie with Georgia and Alex—it was that it was weird watching a steamy one with them after what happened last night. While Alex and I had a very colorful college life together, none of that ever crossed over into his relationship with Georgia. We might have shared a lot of things over the years, but she hadn't been one of them.

That was why I'd found it hard to look at her all day when I couldn't get the sight of her face as she came out of my head. I hadn't meant to catch Alex going down on her, but when I did, I also hadn't been able to look away. I knew I needed to, but the sight of her coming undone right beside me as my best friend ate her pussy did something to me that I hadn't been able to process. I had always found Georgia attractive from the first time I met her, but she had always been off-limits because she was with Alex.

The moaning on the TV continued as I heard Georgia and Alex whispering. I hated feeling like the third wheel with nowhere else to go. I could tough it out and go hang out by myself in the living room, but I didn't want to make things worse, given how much Alex was stressed about the repairs that needed to be done. Had we known what we were walking into, we probably wouldn't have come up this weekend to try to get the work started. Now, we were stuck waiting out a blizzard while sharing the only functional bedroom and bathroom in the cabin.

"I'm going to go make some popcorn and get a refill," Alex said as he climbed out of bed. "Anyone want anything?"

Georgia was in the middle between us but kept her attention on her husband and continued to avoid me like she had most of the day.

I didn't have any plans to get drunk, but a drink to numb me for a bit sounded pretty good.

"I'll take a refill," I said as I started to get up to grab my glass from the dresser beneath the TV.

There wasn't much room for the nightstands once the other bed was brought in, so I'd been using the dresser to hold the few things I had.

"I got it," he said, waving for me to sit down as he grabbed my glass and headed to the kitchen.

Another sex scene came on, and I groaned in frustration when the sounds of moaning filled the air.

"Not a fan of the *Fifty Shades* movies," Georgia asked with a hint of teasing in her tone.

I propped up on my side and looked at her with one eyebrow raised to keep from looking at the TV.

"I think your husband is trying to torture me by playing it," I admitted.

Alex mentioned to me that Georgia had caught me watching them last night when we went to the store. I knew she had, and I knew she would tell Alex because she wouldn't want to keep something like that from him. But Georgia and I hadn't talked about it yet, which made this even more awkward. It would be typical for Alex to put this movie on just to make me squirm until I grew the balls to talk to Georgia and clear the air between us.

"Actually, I picked it," Georgia said, hiccupping as she smiled.

I could tell that she was slightly buzzed from the wine she'd had at dinner. She had declined Alex's offer for a refill when we came into the bedroom to watch a movie. It wasn't like there was anything else to do in the cabin since this was the only room that had heat.

"Oh," I replied before I quickly snapped my mouth shut and tried to smile at her.

"I know you saw us last night. And I know you know that I know because Alex said that you knew, and he knew you wouldn't say anything until you knew that I knew."

I raised an eyebrow at her as the corners of my lips turned into a smile.

"Is this your version of the episode of Friends where they don't know we know they know, or something like that?" I teased, not addressing the topic we actually needed to.

"Maybe," she admitted with another hiccup. "But the point is that we all know, so you can stop acting all weird about it."

I laughed as I sat up and pointed a finger at my chest.

"*I'm* acting weird? What about you earlier when you couldn't even stand to be in the same room as me?"

She shrugged as she leaned against the padded headboard and smiled.

"That was before I had wine."

"So, what you're saying is that I have to keep you liquored up all weekend?"

I hadn't heard Alex's footsteps as he came down the hall and entered the room.

"Why are we keeping my wife all liquored up this weekend?" he asked as he handed me my glass while carefully balancing the bowl of popcorn and his glass.

"We're not," I said a little too nervously.

He raised an eyebrow and called me on my bullshit.

"Dex wants to keep me all liquored up so I won't make him feel weird about watching me come."

"That's not—" I started to object before Alex cut me off.

"That's just because he's jealous that he wasn't the one to make you come on his tongue," Alex said, plopping down on the bed beside Georgia after handing her the bowl of popcorn.

"Is that it? Are you jealous?" Georgia asked, tilting her head to the side as she popped a piece of popcorn in between her plump lips.

I shook my head, trying to clear whatever daydream I was in because there was absolutely no way my best friend and his wife were sitting here talking about me eating her pussy like it was an everyday conversation.

"I don't even know how to answer that," I admitted, throwing my hands in the air.

"Relax, I'm just teasing," Georgia said, reaching over to smack my arm.

That was how close we were to each other, and how close she was last night when I saw her climax.

"But if you change your mind, just let us know," Alex teased, pulling Georgia into his side as the movie continued playing.

I knew they were just fucking with me as I took a long swig and felt the burn as the whiskey slid down my throat. I wasn't buzzed, but I was feeling good, which was usually a bad thing when it came to Alex and me. Instead of talking each other off ledges, we'd see how far we could get the other to jump, like with him joking about me going down on Georgia.

"I'm always down to eat some pussy," I said, chewing my lower lip as both of their heads turned in my direction.

Georgia's face flushed the prettiest shade of red as Alex's smirk grew. That fucker knew exactly what he was doing when he started pushing me. Little did he know that when it came to Georgia, all bets were off.

<u>S</u>even
Georgia

My face was still flaming red as I stared at Dex, my jaw hanging wide open.

Did he seriously just say that he's always down to eat pussy? Like it's the equivalent of ordering food? Oh, yeah, I think I'll take a large pussy with extra sauce and pepperoni...

I shook my head as I tried to figure out what was happening. I knew the few glasses of wine I had were giving me a nice buzz, but this was way past that. This was like stepping into an alternate universe where my husband and his best friend were both looking at me as if I were a piece of meat, and they hadn't eaten in weeks.

"If you keep sitting there with your mouth open like that, I'm going to tell Dex to stick his cock in it," Alex said, running his finger down the length of my arm.

I turned my head and studied him, wondering if maybe *he* was the one who had too much to drink.

Both of them were barely on their second glass of whiskey, and Alex had nursed his first one for well over an hour, so I couldn't imagine it was him being drunk. Maybe there was something with the altitude making them sick? I'd heard of altitude sickness, but I never bothered to learn more about it, given that it never seemed like something I would have to worry about.

"Can't say I would mind that," Dex said, lifting his glass to his lips and taking a sip as I studied his every single move.

His eyes locked onto mine as he lowered the glass and licked his lips slowly.

My eyebrows raised in utter surprise as I felt Alex's hand wrap around my waist before his fingers skimmed the skin at the bottom of my shirt.

What in the world was happening right now?

I took a long, slow, deep breath in and held it. Maybe I just needed oxygen. Perhaps I was forgetting to breathe, and my brain was conjuring up these wild fantasies.

But when I slowly let it out, I felt Alex's hand as it slid up my shirt across my stomach, where it hovered just beneath my breasts that suddenly felt heavy.

"Am I dreaming?" I asked uncertainly, not to anyone in particular.

"No, but that doesn't mean we can't make that dream you had the other night come true," Alex whispered before biting the bottom of my ear playfully.

I turned and looked at him, completely embarrassed that he would bring it up with Dex. But then again, why be embarrassed now when he was challenging his friend to eat my pussy and offering me to give him a blow job?

"Given how much you're blushing, I think I want all of the details of that dream," Dex said, lying on the bed lazily as if this wasn't the most insane thing in the world to be happening right now.

The movie continued playing, and I blocked out the sound of her moaning as I focused on what was happening before me.

"It was nothing," I lied, my body jerking against Alex's as his fingers moved higher, trailing over my breasts. He nudged my head to the side, forcing my neck to be extended as he began kissing it. He knew how much it turned me on to be kissed there, which meant I was literally melting into his touch as he continued.

"It wasn't nothing," Alex objected, pulling his mouth from my skin briefly to talk. "Tell us, and maybe we can make it happen, Georgia. It's all whatever *you* want. Whatever makes you comfortable and leaves you satisfied."

"Can we just stop for a minute and talk about whatever the hell this is?" I demanded, pulling away from his touch so my brain wouldn't be as foggy. Whatever effects the wine had on me were now gone as well.

"Of course," Alex said, folding his hands in his lap.

I glanced down, noticing the bulge that wasn't there a few minutes ago. I arched an eyebrow in question, but he just shrugged.

"You can't blame me for getting turned on about thoughts of you with my best friend," he replied with a smile.

"But it's *Dex*," I whispered, though it was loud enough to be a shout. I pointed behind me to where he was, refusing to look at him while I had this conversation with my husband.

"I am sitting right here, you know," Dex replied lazily as if he wasn't bothered by this conversation at all.

I took a deep breath and closed my eyes as I let it out, rolling my head on my neck to try to relieve some of the mounting tension.

"The past few years in our marriage, you've talked about your fantasy of being with two guys at the same time," Alex said matter-of-factly. "I'm just saying that it doesn't have to stay a fantasy if you don't want it to."

"But it's Dex!" I repeated, this time full-on shouting it. "He's your best friend!"

"I would like to think that I'm *your* best friend as well," Dex said, sending goosebumps over my skin with the way he said it.

"Exactly. He's *our* best friend," Alex amended. "Which means that I trust him not to do anything to hurt you. If we decide to open our marriage to another person, I can't think of anyone better than Dex."

"I can't even begin to think through this right now," I replied, shaking my head as I looked between them. "I'm going to take a bath."

I scooted down the bed, not wanting to climb over my husband, who still had a bulge in his sweats, and locked myself in the bathroom.

Eight
Alex

"I should have asked before I did that," I said to Dex once I heard the water running in the bathroom. I knew Georgia just needed some time to wrap her head around everything, and then she would be open to discussing this with me. But with Dex, I didn't want to make him uncomfortable if I had misread the situation.

"Did what? Offer me up to be the third wheel in your marriage?" he asked with a smirk.

"You are never the third wheel. You know that."

"No, but I think we do need to discuss the logistics of this *if* it's something she wants to consider."

"I agree," I said, nodding my head. "Georgia just needs some time to think about everything, then we'll talk."

"And you're sure this is something she wants?"

"I'm pretty sure. She's mentioned it so many times when we have sex that I know it's a fantasy of hers. I didn't realize until last night that she actually had someone she was picturing when we talked about having another man involved when we had sex."

Dex looked at me with uncertainty in his eyes, which left an uneasy feeling in my stomach.

"Georgia was upset this morning that you saw us last night. When I talked to her about it and mentioned how she has fantasies like that, she got really embarrassed in a way I hadn't seen from her before. I asked her if it was you she had been thinking of during these fantasies, and she wouldn't answer. But her blush gave her away."

"I love when she blushes," Dex admitted. "But then again, I love everything about Georgia. I don't want to do anything that will jeopardize our friendship."

"I don't either. I'm not willing to lose either of you."

"Aren't you worried that we're risking that if we cross this line? It's not like when we were in college, and we'd fuck around with the same girl. This is your wife." He pinned me with a look that made me swallow hard.

"I know. And I don't know. I have no idea what will happen if we cross this line. I just know that my wife wants more than what I can give her, and I hate that. If she wants to fulfill some fantasy by having another man in bed with us, I'm okay with that. But I would feel better if I knew that person. I don't want it to be some scumbag who hurts her. I want it to be someone who will love and respect her the way I do."

"I would never hurt Georgia," Dex said softly, looking from me to the TV where the movie had ended.

"I know. I also don't want to risk you getting hurt in any of this either."

"I'm a big boy," he replied, rubbing his lips together as he smirked.

Dex and I had never been intimate with each other, but that didn't mean we hadn't seen each other's cocks. It was impossible not to when you're fucking the same girl at the same time, and everyone is trying to figure out who goes in which hole. Needless to say, I knew what he would be bringing to the proverbial table if Georgia decided to go through with this.

"Well, it will all be up to Georgia and whatever she decides," I said, knowing she was likely doing anything but relaxing in the bath as her mind went a mile a minute thinking about this.

"It goes without saying that I'll give her whatever her heart desires. There's nothing I wouldn't do for Georgia."

My lips turned upward into a smile as I heard the love in my best friend's voice for my wife.

Nine
Georgia

I sank lower into the water, allowing the heat to penetrate the tight muscles in my shoulders. I would kill for a massage, but it never failed that when Alex gave me one, it always led to more. Not that I was complaining—but it was a little hard to have sex with my husband, given everything going on with Dex.

My mind was still reeling from the conversation about Dex joining us. I knew Alex was okay with it because he never would have mentioned it if he wasn't. But I was genuinely surprised by how interested Dex seemed to be. While I had been having fantasies about him all along, I never expected he might feel the same about me. We'd always had very clear boundaries that none of us had crossed until now.

I took a deep breath and let it out slowly when I heard a knock on the bathroom door.

"Hey, sorry to bother you, but I really gotta take a piss," Dex said tightly. "I would go outside, but the snow is blocking the door, and it's too dark to try to clear it."

"Ummm… yeah. Give me a second," I called out as I reached up and grabbed the shower curtain, pulling it as hard as I could without yanking it down.

The bathroom was decent-sized, but it only had a shower/tub combo, which I didn't mind. At least this way, I could give him privacy to use the restroom without having to give up my bath.

"Okay. You can come in."

The door opened and then closed as I heard his soft footsteps approach.

"I'm sorry. I've been trying to hold it, but someone decided we should have another drink, and now I think I'm going to explode," Dex explained.

"It's not a problem. Sorry I'm taking so long."

I made the mistake of glancing through the small gap where the shower curtain didn't cover and studied Dex's muscular back as he relieved himself.

"You never need to apologize for that, Georgia," he replied, looking over his shoulder and catching me staring.

My eyes traveled up to his, and a flush of heat rushed through me. There was something different in how he looked at me, and suddenly, I wanted more. I broke his gaze as my eyes ventured down his body to where his hand was still holding his cock.

I knew I was playing with fire, but I didn't care. Curiosity was getting the best of me, and even though I had been flustered when Alex brought up the idea of Dex joining us, I hadn't been able to stop obsessing over it.

"Can I see it?" I asked, the words immediately sending a rush of excitement and nervousness through me at the same time. *Why the fuck did I just ask that?!*

My mind had been so focused on the idea of something happening between us that I failed to stop and realize where and what we were doing when I asked.

He arched an eyebrow and then slowly turned to me, holding his cock in his hand.

Instinctively, I licked my lips, knowing how good it would feel. He wasn't even hard, and yet it was huge, thick, and veiny.

I continued staring as he gripped it and began stroking himself as my eyes stayed glued to it. I could come just from watching him jack himself off, and that was a scary thought. Aside from Alex, there was no one who could get me off that easily, but Dex was looking like a sure thing. There was this energy that swarmed my body, making me feel alive and on fire at the same time, and I wanted more of it.

"It's yours if you want it, Georgia," he said softly, continuing to slide his hand up and down the shaft as he got harder.

My eyes flashed up to his, knowing that this wasn't a game. I wasn't just fantasizing about him anymore. This was reality if I wanted it to be.

I opened my mouth to speak, but shut it when he smiled and winked at me before tucking it inside his sweats. He flushed the toilet and then washed his hands.

"Just let me know," he threw over his shoulder as he opened the door and walked out, closing it behind him.

I blew out a heavy breath and sank under the water, allowing it to cover my face while I considered his offer.

Ten

Alex

I was lying on the bed, trying to stay awake, when Georgia finished her bath and came into the bedroom. Her hair was down and wet as she combed through it. She was wearing the same shirt she wore last night to bed, and I knew she felt comfortable in it. She was not as comfortable as she would be in the one she always wore at home, but I understood she wasn't ready for Dex to see her like that yet.

It was clear that the three of us were interested in exploring things between us, but I didn't want to push Georgia into it. I wanted her to be the one to initiate things so Dex and I could follow at her pace. If we had it our way, she would be spread out on the bed while we took turns feasting on her.

"I'm going to go fix a snack," Dex said, shoving off the bed and walking out of the room, leaving us alone.

Once he was gone, Georgia stood next to me, leaned down, and whispered in my ear.

"I saw his cock."

I fought the grin that wanted to spread across my face as I slowly looked up at her. She looked adorable with her cheeks stained red and her green eyes dilated.

"Sorry, baby. I know it's hard with only one bathroom right now," I said cautiously, not wanting to accuse her of anything until I knew exactly what had happened.

"No!" she whispered louder, her eyes widening as she glanced at the door. "I asked him to see it."

I chuckled but tried to hide it with a cough.

"You asked Dex to see his cock?"

She nodded, chewing her lower lip as she held the comb in her hand.

"Okay. And he let you?"

She nodded again, but I failed to see what the problem was.

"Did he not want to show you?"

"I don't know. He didn't seem mad about it. I wasn't trying to look, but there was a gap that the shower curtain didn't cover when I tried to pull it closed, so I saw him standing there, holding it, and I knew he wasn't trying to do anything but use the restroom, but I couldn't just stop thinking about it—"

"Breathe, baby," I said, standing up and putting my hands on her hips.

She took a deep breath in and slowly released it. I was more worried she would pass out from lack of oxygen trying to get all of that out than I was about her asking to see his cock.

"Do you think he is upset with me?" she asked, scrunching her face.

"No. Why would he be?"

"I don't know, Alex," she replied, throwing her hands in the air while maintaining her grip on the comb. "Because I asked to see his cock while he was just in there to take a piss?"

"You always ask to see mine when I take one when you soak at home," I said gently.

"That's different. You're my husband."

"Well, we'll just call it the bath tax." I grinned, loving the way her features changed from flustered to confused.

"What are you talking about?"

"A bath tax. Whenever one of us interrupts your soaking time in the bath to take a piss, we'll pay a bath tax and show you our cocks."

"How often do you think this is going to happen?" She placed her hand on her hip and stared at me.

"Well, given that you like to soak a few times a week at home, and we're likely stuck here for a few weeks, I would say a handful."

"You're not helping," she hissed, smacking my chest with the comb.

"I'm sorry," I said with a soft laugh as I pulled her into my arms and hugged her. "I was just trying to make you feel better."

"Thank you. I appreciate that. But we have bigger problems here that we can't just ignore."

"And what's that, baby?"

She tipped her head back and stared at the ceiling as if saying a silent prayer. Then she lowered her head and stared me in the eyes.

"I liked it."

My heart raced as I processed what she was saying.

"What do you want to do about it?"

"I don't know," she replied nervously, lifting her hand to chew her nail. "We've crossed so many lines already that I don't know if we can go back to how things used to be."

I shrugged, not sure if she wanted me to answer that or if she just wanted to get the thoughts out of her head.

"He told me that it's mine if I want it…"

I arched an eyebrow and tilted my head to study her.

"Do you want it?"

She nodded and quickly tried to look away as I gently reached up and placed my hand on the side of her face to stop her.

"Okay. If that's what you want, then we'll make it happen."

"Just like that?"

"Like what?"

"I say that I want to have sex with your best friend, and you're okay with it?"

"Yeah, Georgia. I'm more than okay with it. I know Dex and trust him. I can see the chemistry between the two of you, and I think that as long as this is something everyone wants, then why not? We're all consenting adults."

"Do you think he's really going to go through with this?"

"There's only one way to find out."

She took a deep breath and slowly let it out.

"Why don't I go make us some food, and the three of us can sit down and talk about it?"

"Okay. I like that idea."

I leaned in and placed a kiss on her forehead, loving the way she melted into my touch.

Eleven

Dex

I stayed in the kitchen longer than necessary to give Alex and Georgia a few minutes alone. I could only imagine how frustrating it must have been for her not to have any privacy to talk to her husband, especially given everything that had happened tonight.

I closed the fridge, frustrated when I couldn't find anything I wanted to eat. The house was fully stocked with groceries after we went to the store earlier, but the one thing I wanted to eat was currently in the bedroom with her husband. I shoved a hand through my hair and let out a groan as I thought about how difficult this was going to be.

If Georgia said yes to trying something like this, that would be great, until it wasn't. No matter how hard we tried, there would be no way to keep everyone from getting hurt. Someone was bound to regardless of what we did.

But also knowing that Georgia was interested and maybe didn't want to go through with any of it was just as hard because the line between us had already been crossed. Not only had I offered to eat her pussy, I had shown her my cock in the bathroom and stroked myself while I pictured doing it.

Things were getting complicated and fast.

I opened the pantry and looked inside, still frustrated that I couldn't find anything to satisfy the craving I had. I wasn't so much hungry as I was horny and frustrated, but it wasn't like there was anywhere in the cabin where I could relieve myself without Alex and Georgia knowing what I was doing. I hadn't even touched her yet, and I was a complete mess.

I shut the door and sat down at the table, holding my head in my hands as I stared at the old wood beneath me.

"She got to you already," Alex said, entering the kitchen and startling me.

"What?" I looked up to find him opening the fridge and pulling out stuff for breakfast. I glanced at the clock on the wall, noting that it was barely after eleven. It didn't surprise me that he was making her favorite food in the middle of the night because there wasn't anything he wouldn't do for her.

"Georgia thinks best when she's had a solid meal," he explained without looking at me. "I don't know about you, but I can't go a few weeks cooped up in this cabin with all of this tension surrounding us. So, I'm going to make breakfast, and then we're all going to sit down and talk."

"Does Georgia know this?" I asked, turning my body to face him.

"Georgia knows everything," she said with a smile as she walked into the kitchen wearing my t-shirt.

I didn't want to admit how much it bothered me that she was wearing it because it wasn't that I was upset about it— it was that I loved her in it more than I should. She pulled at the hem, tugging it down as if she knew what I was thinking.

"That she does," Alex agreed as he set several pans on the burners and began cooking.

Georgia came and sat beside me, looking up at me nervously beneath her thick lashes. I gave her a warm smile and felt the weird butterflies I got every time she returned it.

"Do you need help?" I asked Alex, needing something to keep me occupied as my knee bounced under the table.

"I've got it, but thanks."

I nodded and rubbed my lips together, stopping suddenly when I felt Georgia's hand touch me beneath the table. She stared at me as she rested her hand on my knee, stopping it from bouncing. I reached down and rested my hand on hers, giving it a gentle squeeze.

"Georgia and I talked in the bedroom while you were in here looking for a snack, and we both agree that we don't want to do anything to make things weird for any of us," Alex said as he used tongs to flip the bacon that was already sizzling in the pan.

Georgia nodded and gave me another soft smile.

"I don't want things to be weird for any of us either," I agreed, fighting the urge to get up and pace the kitchen. I was wound tight and full of energy with no way to expel it, or at least not in an appropriate way.

Alex flipped the bacon again and then cracked a few eggs into another pan. I knew Georgia's favorite meal was bacon and scrambled eggs, so it didn't surprise me that he was making them for her. It surprised me more how much I knew about someone who wasn't *my* wife. He sprinkled some salt and pepper over the eggs and then pushed them around with the spatula as they cooked.

A few minutes later, he brought Georgia's food over to the table and set it in front of her as he placed a kiss on the top of her head. Then he returned with our food, setting our plates down before grabbing the jug of orange juice from the fridge.

"Thank you for making breakfast," Georgia said as she smiled up at him.

"Anything for you, my love."

I looked away and took a bite of my eggs, not caring that they were still hot and burned my throat as I swallowed them. Maybe a little bit of pain was what I needed to keep me distracted.

"Okay," Alex blurted out with a heavy sigh. "We have food, we have orange juice, now let's talk."

"You make it sound so formal," Georgia responded with a nervous laugh.

"That's because it is. Once we talk through the details of everything and make sure we're all on the same page, then we can move on to the fun stuff. However, I don't think any of us can do that until we discuss things as a group. We can't beat around the bush with something like this. We have to be fully open and honest, or this will never work." Alex squeezed her hand as she nodded.

"Dex, you know that I love my wife more than anything in this world, and her happiness is my top priority," he said, looking at me before glancing at Georgia. "We've discussed inviting another man into our bedroom, but you're the only one either of us would trust enough with something like this."

"I agree," Georgia said, turning to face me. "Dex, you're the only one I want to do this with. But there's no pressure to cross this line with us. I respect our friendship, but more importantly, I respect the friendship that the two of you have. I would not want my fantasies to jeopardize that."

My eyebrows raised on their own as my two best friends looked at me.

"I am flattered that you guys would consider me. I am also open to discussing all of this."

"I know that things are different for you, Dex, with you being single. I don't want you to feel like you're jumping into a relationship with us if you do this. But I think it's important that we know beforehand if you plan to continue dating, just so we can all make sure we know what's going on."

"No," I said quickly, shaking my head as I noticed the look of worry and hurt that crossed Georgia's face briefly before she pushed it away. "I don't have any plans or desire to see anyone else."

"Perfect. I think we can absolutely make whatever this ends up being between the three of us work. As with any relationship—friendship or romantic—communication is key. I know that I'm comfortable talking about anything with both of you, but I want to make sure that you guys feel comfortable talking to each other as well. If something is happening between the two of you, I want to know that you'll be able to talk about it and deal with it without risking your friendship."

"I'm willing to do that," Georgia said, looking at me.

"I would never hurt you, Georgia," I admitted, keeping her gaze. "You have my promise that I will always talk to both of you about anything that's going on. There won't be any secrets being kept on my end from you guys."

"See, I told you everything would be fine once we talked about it," Alex said gently to Georgia.

"I know, but we still haven't talked about *the other stuff*," she replied.

"The sex?" I offered, raising my eyebrows.

She blushed as she looked down and focused on her plate, avoiding eye contact.

"If this is going to work, that includes being able to look at me when I mention the word sex," I teased playfully, nudging her shoulder with mine.

I waited until she finally looked up at me before continuing.

"There you go. That's what I'm talking about. I want your full attention when I tell you things like how much I want to eat your pussy or how good I imagine your lips will feel wrapped around my cock."

"Her pussy is quite delicious. You're gonna love it. And I agree, her mouth is pure perfection when she gives head," Alex said, his eyes focused on his wife as she shifted between us, letting out a heavy sigh.

"You two are going to be the death of me, aren't you?" Georgia asked, lifting her head as she took turns looking at us.

"Oh, baby. You have no idea what's in store for you," Alex said, his voice dropping slightly. "What Dex and I will do to you will leave you begging for more. If you thought my cock was good, wait until you have both."

"At the same time?" Georgia asked right as I took a bite and immediately began choking.

"Possibly," Alex replied easily. "But we'll work you up to that. We'll start slow and then see what you like and what you don't like."

"Will you two… You know…" Her eyes widened as she refused to finish her sentence.

"No. Dex and I have no desire to fuck each other, Georgia."

"Oh. Okay." She let out a shaky breath as I stared at my best friend and shook my head.

What did I just agree to?

Twelve
Georgia

"Take him deeper, baby. Let Dex feel how good your pussy feels wrapped around his cock," Alex coaxed as I nodded my head and lifted my butt so Dex could slide in further.

"Fuck," I cried, gripping the sheets beneath me as a burning sensation spread across my vagina as he stretched me further.

"Are you okay?" Dex asked, stopping as he hovered above me with his hands braced beside my head.

"Yeah," I breathed out heavily. "I didn't expect you to be so big."

"We can stop if you want to."

"No. Don't even think about it," I warned, trying to steady my breathing as I shifted slightly and felt him slide in deeper.

He tilted his head back and closed his eyes, exposing the muscles in his neck and shoulders as he struggled not to come yet.

Alex lay beside us as he stroked his cock, watching as his best friend fucked me.

I moaned, desperate for the relief I knew was coming. I was so full, and my clit hummed with need as Dex brushed a finger over it.

"Georgia," someone whispered, trying to interrupt my dream.

I shook my head, refusing to wake up. I could feel the ache deep inside my pussy and was on the verge of coming. I just needed a few more minutes to get there. I arched my back and felt something hard against my ass. I didn't have to open my eyes to know it was Alex's cock as I reached back and stroked it with the palm of my hand through his boxer briefs. I must have been grinding on it in my sleep and woke him up.

The only problem was that he wasn't wearing boxer briefs. The fabric was thicker and covered him and his massive erection almost as if he were wearing—

Fuck. My eyes shot open as I quickly turned my head to see Dex behind me, staring at me with something I hadn't seen before. Was that lust? His eyes were dilated, and his lips were moist from where he had just licked them as his hand rested on my hip.

My hand was still pressed against the fabric of his sweats as his cock twitched beneath it.

I quickly pulled it back, covering my mouth when I looked over to find Alex on his back, asleep.

"I'm so sorry," I whispered, trying not to wake my husband as I attempted to pull away from Dex.

His grip tightened, holding me in place.

"You don't need to apologize. But I swear, if you don't start telling me about these dreams, I'm going to lose my mind."

I chewed my lower lip as I looked up at him, wondering how much I had said or if I had just been moaning like last night.

"Apparently, I'm a little worked up these days, and my subconscious is trying to take care of it," I teased quietly.

"Make her come," Alex said, still lying on his back with his eyes closed. His voice was gruff, still thick with sleep.

I opened my mouth, trying to think of what to say. I didn't mean to do anything, but at the same time, we had just finished talking about the three of us doing stuff together, so it wasn't like I was going behind his back.

"Stop overthinking it, Georgia. You're horny and rightfully so. Let Dex make you come so you sleep better."

"Are you going to be mad?" I asked, hating the uncertainty in my voice. It wasn't even like Dex had said he wanted to do this. It was just Alex volunteering him to.

"Not at all, baby. I'm going to rest because when we get up in a few hours, I'm going to fuck you long and hard until you can't come anymore. Then, when I'm done, Dex is going to fuck you and worship that tight little pussy of yours."

I nodded even though I knew he couldn't see me. While he had given us his blessing, I didn't want to take advantage of the situation. How was I supposed to even start a conversation with Dex? *Hey, my husband knows that I'm horny and two seconds from humping a pillow to get relief, so do you mind if I use your hands or face to get off?*

"Stop overthinking it," Dex said softly, echoing what Alex just said as he trailed his finger from my shoulder down the side of my arm. "If you want me to take care of you, I'm more than happy to. Just tell me what you want, Georgia."

"Oh, no. It's fine. Really. It's late and we don't need to—"

Before I could finish my sentence, Dex flipped me onto my back and leaned over me, gently pressing his lips to mine. My body melted beneath his as I parted my lips and allowed his tongue to swipe over mine.

"There's not a time in the day or night when you need something that I won't give it to you," he said sternly, breaking the kiss as his lips feathered over my ear. "Now be a good girl and tell me what you need—my mouth or my fingers."

There was no way this was really happening. I closed my eyes and tilted my neck as he kissed it, biting a few times as he waited for my answer. Having his hard, muscular body on top of mine while he kissed my neck and called me a good girl was almost my undoing.

"I'm waiting, Georgia," he warned, sliding his hand up until it was wrapped snugly around my throat.

Fuck me.

My body was on fire as he put more pressure, completely soaking my panties from how aroused I was. I never knew I would be this turned on from something like this, but it was hot as fuck. Alex and I role-played often, but we hadn't done this before. Or maybe it was because it was Dex and not Alex—almost a forbidden fruit kind of thing.

"Both," I whimpered, panting for more as he released my throat.

His hand moved over my breast, palming it through the fabric of his T-shirt before slipping it beneath the fabric.

"Fuck, I love seeing you wear this," he said. "But it needs to come off."

I sat up as he lifted it over my head and tossed it to the floor, leaving me completely on display without a bra and only my cotton panties.

He gently pushed me back onto the bed as he held himself above me, rubbing his erection against my pussy while pulling a pebbled nipple into his mouth. The friction from the fabric rubbed in all the right places, but I wanted more. Needed more. Dry humping was great, but I wanted to feel him inside of me without all of these barriers.

I reached up and grabbed the back of his head, holding him in place as he sucked harder, making me squirm as I whimpered. He lifted slightly until he lowered his hand and brushed it against my thigh. He was taking his time, which was nice, but I felt like I was on the verge of exploding if I didn't come soon.

His fingers feathered over my panties, pushing them to the side as they skimmed over my slit.

"Fuck, Georgia. You're so wet," he growled as he lay beside me, his erection resting against my thigh.

He slid a finger inside, parting me easily through the arousal that had coated my panties. I arched my back, bringing my breasts closer to his face as he began sucking the other nipple, pulling it between his teeth for a second as he bit it.

"Ahhh," I cried, not able to be quiet with how he was torturing my body right now.

I heard Alex chuckle as he continued to lie there, giving us a bit of privacy by not watching. But I knew he was fully awake and listening to all of this.

Dex added two more fingers until he was fucking me with three, his hand completely soaked.

"Please, Dex," I begged, writhing beneath him as I moved my hips to try to force his hand to rub my clit. "Make me come."

He kissed my lips hard and quickly before he lowered himself between my legs and removed my panties. They got tossed to the floor with his shirt as he grabbed my thighs and positioned them on his shoulders. The sight of him between my legs immediately reminded me of my dream and nearly sent me over the edge.

His fingers stayed inside of me, stimulating my G-spot as he flicked my clit with his tongue. He was teasing me in the worst way as he slowly pulled it into his mouth and sucked.

I gripped the sheets beneath me as I tried to hold on, but there was no use. Dex absolutely knew what he was doing as he pressed one hand firmly on my lower stomach while pressing his fingers against my G-spot. I squirmed, feeling the buildup as he increased the pressure until a rush of fluid came squirting out of me and directly into his mouth.

I panted, struggling to catch my breath as I expected him to stop but he just removed his fingers and used both hands to pin my hips down as his mouth focused on my clit.

"I can't," I whimpered. "I can't come again."

He lifted his head for a second, making eye contact with me before he spoke.

"I'm not stopping until you give me every last bit."

"But I can't. I don't have anything left," I objected, my body already feeling tired.

"Come for me, Georgia. I want to feel your pussy as it spasms against my tongue and lips while I suck every ounce of your arousal up."

His dirty words were exactly what sent me over the final edge as he pulled my clit in between his lips and sucked until I felt the waves of pleasure wash over me as I came.

Thirteen

Dex

I was a fucking goner.

Georgia tasted like summertime mixed with fresh laundry and rain—all of my favorite things. But it wasn't just tasting her that had gotten to me. It was feeling how her body reacted to my touch.

I was deep asleep when I felt her plump ass grind against my cock, stirring it awake. All it took was the scent of her shampoo as she rested her head against my chest for her to imprint on me. Okay, so we weren't teenagers and this wasn't a vampire romance, but I swear to God I never felt anything like what happened when that line with Georgia was crossed. It was like I stepped into a brand new world, and I was never going back.

Her body was pure perfection with full, heavy tits that begged to be sucked and a tight pussy I couldn't wait to fuck. But none of that was as good as knowing that I got her off so good she couldn't move after. Alex laughed as he got up and grabbed a wet washcloth to clean her up with, but by the time he got back, she was already snoring.

"Sorry she left you high and dry," he teased after tossing the washcloth to the floor with the other stuff. I would clean it all up in the morning, but for now, I just wanted my dick to go down and get some rest.

"Are you sure you're okay with what just happened?" I asked, sitting on the edge of the bed as he covered Georgia with a blanket before he sat beside me.

"I am. I think this was bound to happen, given how close we all are and that there's a mutual attraction. Georgia and I have talked about this many times, both during sex and outside of the bedroom. I know how much it turns her on to be with another man. I'm glad that it's someone we both trust."

"But what about you? It doesn't bother you seeing me go down on her?"

"Honestly, I didn't watch. But that was only because I wanted her to have her space without worrying about what I thought. But to answer the question you're really trying to ask, no, it doesn't bother me sharing her with you. Just don't hurt her."

"I would never," I rushed out, stopping when he held his hand up.

"I know. That's the only reason I'm allowing this to happen."

"If it gets weird, you'll tell me, right?"

"Absolutely. I appreciate your concern, but given our past experiences with sharing other women, I'm not at all worried about things getting weird between you and me. I know what kind of person you are, and I am one thousand percent comfortable welcoming you into our bed. My main concern is Georgia and making sure this is what she wants since she's never done this before. We'll see how she feels about it in a few hours when she gets up. Get some rest. We have our work cut out for us tomorrow with clearing the snow from the house."

I nodded and gave Georgia a final glance before I lay down and faced the wall, hoping sleep would come easily once my cock calmed down.

The next morning, Georgia and Alex were already awake and making breakfast when I got up. I jumped in the shower and allowed the hot water to soothe me as I worried about seeing Georgia after what happened last night. I hoped she didn't regret it because I sure as fuck didn't, but who knew how she would feel about it this morning?

I walked into the kitchen and tried to force a smile when I saw her sitting on the counter with Alex between her legs as he kissed her neck.

"The pancakes are going to burn," she giggled before she looked up and spotted me. "Hey, Dex."

"Good morning," I replied, clearing my throat as I pulled a chair out and sat at the table.

Alex turned and gave me a head nod before returning his focus to the food.

"I can't believe it's still snowing," Georgia said as she looked out the window. "I thought the worst of the storm already happened?"

"According to the news this morning, we haven't seen anything yet. We're supposed to get ten to twelve inches tonight."

I studied Georgia's face as a thought crossed it.

"So we're really not getting off this mountain before Christmas, are we?" she asked, looking at Alex.

"I'm sorry, baby. Probably not." He squeezed her knee gently before turning the burner off and sliding the last few pancakes onto a plate.

"It is what it is. Nothing we can do about it now."

I hated hearing the disappointment in her voice. I knew that neither of them had family in town, so we usually spent the holidays together, just the three of us. But I also knew how much Georgia loved to decorate the house, and she couldn't do that if she were stuck up here.

I got up from the table and walked to the coat rack by the front door, grabbing my jacket and throwing it on as I headed into the blistery cold without looking back.

Fourteen

Alex

"Hey, everything alright?" I asked Dex as I caught up to him at the shed across from the house.

The wind howled as it whipped past us, sending a cloud of snow into the air.

He glanced over his shoulder, noticing me standing there as he shoved his weight into the door, forcing it open. We stepped inside, and I grabbed the block my grandfather always used to hold it open. The last thing I needed was for us to get stuck inside the shed with no way to get out, leaving Georgia to fend for herself during the blizzard.

"I could swear I saw some Christmas stuff in here when your grandmother showed us around over the summer," he answered, shoving a few boxes to the side so he could see the shelves.

We had intended to do the work for her over the summer, but then she got ill and everything got pushed back. We kept waiting for her to get better, but that never happened. She went from being an independent woman who could do things on her own to needing to be in assisted living.

"Great minds think alike," I replied with a smile. "I was planning to come and look after breakfast."

"Sorry, I didn't mean to interrupt your breakfast. I just couldn't stand the disappointment in her voice."

"It's not a big deal. I fixed her plate and told her to start eating. There's probably not much, but I know there's an artificial tree my grandma used to put up every year after my grandpa died. We can start with that and see what else we find."

Dex nodded as he began looking through the different bins on the shelf in front of him, while I looked through the ones on the other side.

"Bingo!" he said with a huge smile as he tilted the box to the side so I could see inside.

There were boxes of ornaments and lights, along with a handful of decorations that I remembered from my childhood.

"Sweet. If you want to grab that, I'll get the tree."

He nodded and put the lid back on before grabbing it and taking it to the door while he waited for me. Thankfully, the tree was easy to spot in the corner of the shed, so I grabbed it and then followed Dex out, making sure to secure the door behind us so it didn't get blown open in the storm.

Georgia was sitting on the couch, eating breakfast, when we returned. Her eyes widened and then narrowed in confusion as we set everything down.

"What's all that?" she asked, setting her plate on the coffee table that desperately needed to be fixed.

"Since we can't go home for Christmas, we're bringing Christmas to you," I announced, turning the tree box to face her so she could see the image.

Her hands went up to her face as she squealed and got up.

"Oh my gosh! Thank you, baby," she said as she leaned up and kissed me. "That means the world to me."

"It was Dex's idea, too."

She smiled softly as she walked over and wrapped her arms around Dex after he set the box down to reciprocate.

"Thank you, Dex," she replied as she looked up at him and brought her lips to his.

I watched as his hands slid around her waist, pulling her tighter to him as she tilted her head and deepened the kiss. I knew it should make me jealous to see my wife kissing another man, but I wasn't. If anything, I was turned on by it. I loved hearing her last night as Dex made her come, and my only regret was that I hadn't watched. But there was plenty of time for that because whatever this thing was, it was just getting started.

Fifteen

Georgia

I sat between Alex and Dex on the bed as we watched another movie. We'd spent the day decorating the house for Christmas, and I was glad they didn't give me any shit about it, given Thanksgiving was only a few days ago. But my love for Christmas was nothing compared to their love for me.

Dex scooted off the bed and went into the bathroom, closing the door behind him. I leaned into Alex's side as his hand wrapped tighter around my waist with his fingers grazing the side of my boob. I giggled and looked up at him, wondering how I had been blessed with such an incredible man as my husband. We hadn't had much time to talk about what happened last night with Dex, but Alex hadn't acted bothered by it at all—especially when he saw Dex kiss me earlier.

"Tell me what you're thinking," Alex said softly.

"I wasn't," I lied, not ready for him to know how deep in my own head I was over everything that was happening.

"You're a terrible liar," he said with a chuckle right as Dex came out of the bathroom.

"What is she lying about?" he asked, climbing onto the bed to resume his seat beside me.

"She's overthinking something, but won't tell me what," Alex replied as if I weren't there and the one they were accusing of lying.

"I'm not—" I started, only to get interrupted by Dex.

"Yeah, I noticed she was deep in her thoughts earlier when she didn't even notice the mistletoe you stuck down your pants."

I opened my mouth to tell them that I never saw such a thing when I felt Dex's heavy gaze on me.

"We could do it again," Alex offered. "See if she notices it this time."

"If you want head, just ask," I said, turning to stare at my husband as desire flooded my body.

"You know what I would love more than the feeling of your soft lips wrapped around my cock?" he asked, lifting my chin with his finger.

"What?"

"Watching you take Dex's cock down your throat while I fuck this sweet pussy and give her the fucking she's been waiting for."

I wanted to say something—anything. To beg for him to put me out of my misery and give me the multiple orgasms I desperately craved. But nothing came out. Instead, I just nodded my head and looked between them as I realized this was really about to happen.

"Such a good girl, isn't she?" Dex commented, his voice low and turning me on even more.

"She is," Alex agreed, stroking his hand down my back. "Why don't you show him how good you can be by sucking his cock?"

I looked up nervously at Dex, unsure how to even begin. With Alex, things were easy because we were comfortable with each other. I could plop down on the floor between his legs and give him head without any cares in the world. But this was Dex… Not only was it Dex—he was my husband's best friend, and I was about to really, *really* see his penis.

Okay, so the word *penis* wasn't all that sexy, but I couldn't focus on any of that as he locked eyes with me and held my gaze while he hooked his fingers into his sweats. Without breaking eye contact, he slowly pulled them down, lifting his hips slightly as he continued lowering them.

I expected there to be some sort of barrier that I would have to go through to see his cock—like underwear—except Dex wasn't wearing any. No, his cock just sat there, jutting straight up already hard as a rock with a dot of precum glistening on the tip.

Fuck. Me.

My panties were already wet before this even started, but at this point, they were soaked. My pussy ached with need as I licked my lips, desperately waiting for permission.

Instead, he continued holding my gaze as he lowered his hand and started stroking himself slowly. I had no idea where his pants went because I had been so distracted by the sight of his cock that everything else was a blur. I hated that he still had his shirt on because the image of him sitting on the bed with those sculpted muscles, as he touched himself, would be high-quality material to store for later.

"He's waiting," Alex said softly as he nudged me.

I looked away from Dex and over my shoulder at my husband, making sure he really was okay with this. He gave me a nod and grinned as he looked past me to where his best friend was waiting. I turned and crawled over to where Dex was sitting with his back leaning against the wall, and looked up at him as I slowly lowered myself between his legs. The look in his eyes nearly set my body on fire with the pure desire evident in them.

Dex stroked himself one last time and slowly pulled his hand away as I replaced it with mine. I licked my lips and then opened my mouth, taking my time as I lowered my head and took him to the back of my throat. I felt his body clench beneath me as his hand gripped the back of my head and held me there.

"Her lips are magical, aren't they?" Alex asked.

I couldn't hear Dex answer, but the way my husband chuckled made me guess that Dex had at least nodded his head. Alex had spent so much time telling Dex how I gave good head, I wasn't going to let him down now.

I gripped the base of his cock with my hand, wrapping it around him as I stroked what didn't fit in my mouth. I wanted to spend hours down there teasing him until I drew every last ounce of pleasure out of him, but the way he was gripping my hair told me he wasn't going to last long, and

I didn't blame him. We were all wound up with so much sexual tension that none of us would. It would be one of those nights where we just focused on getting everyone off so we could tease each other later.

"Fuck," Dex groaned as I pulled back, letting him pop out of my mouth as I licked the tip of his cock. I flicked it a few times before running my tongue on the underside and cupping his balls tightly in my hand. "How do you last that long when she does this?"

I grinned as I twirled my tongue around the tip, teasing him as he let go of my head and gripped the sheets beside me while he struggled to restrain himself.

"She sure knows how to use her mouth," Alex replied with a laugh. "If you think that's bad, just wait until she tightens her pussy around you right before you come."

"Don't talk about her pussy," Dex warned as his head fell back the second I pulled his full length back into my mouth again.

I was wet and aching for a release, but pleasuring Dex was so fucking hot that I didn't want anything else at the moment. I hollowed out my cheeks and sucked as I stroked him hard and fast with my hand, matching the pace I was going with my mouth.

"Fuck. Georgia," Dex panted in warning. "If you don't stop now, I'm going to come down your throat."

I heard Alex chuckle again as if he knew that was exactly what I wanted. I settled in and continued my torture as I sucked until he finally shot ropes of cum down the back of my throat.

Sixteen

Alex

Fuck. That was possibly the hottest fucking thing I had ever seen. I couldn't take my eyes off my wife as she sat there and wiped the corners of her mouth while smirking at my best friend.

I knew she was wet and ready for a release of her own, but I couldn't think about anything other than the raging erection that was begging to be inside of her pussy. I had planned on fucking her from behind while she sucked Dex's cock, but once she got started, I didn't want her to stop. I wanted them to have their moment without us worrying about crossing the line of the three of us doing something together for the first time.

"Did you like sucking his cock?" I asked, pulling her into my arms as she continued to stare at Dex.

"Very much," she replied, finally turning her body and looking at me. "But I'm still waiting for that fucking you keep promising me."

"Trust me, baby, that's the only thing on my mind right now. But first, I want to take care of you."

"I'm fine. Really."

I arched an eyebrow and stared at her, calling her on her bullshit.

"Georgia, if you think that we're not going to take turns making you come, you're seriously mistaken," Dex said.

"I love that—really, I do. But I swear to God, if someone's dick isn't inside of me in the next five minutes…"

"Alright, alright." I shook my head and laughed. "I will fuck you, but you will also let me worship your body along the way. It's been too long since I've been able to touch you, Georgia."

"I know. It's been five days. Five long, frustrating days."

"Well, then, why don't we fix that?"

I leaned down and nudged her head to the side as I slowly kissed the side of her neck. I knew she was horny and wanted sex, but I also wanted this to be all about taking care of her in every way possible.

"Want to help get her undressed?" I asked Dex, pulling my lips away from her skin for a second to speak.

."I'm on it."

Georgia leaned her back against my chest and closed her eyes while I continued kissing her neck and nibbling her ear, while Dex slowly pulled her leggings down. He waited for her to lift her hips before sliding them the rest of the way down, revealing her bare pussy.

"You're not wearing any panties?" I asked, pulling her earlobe between my teeth.

She shook her head and lifted her hand to her mouth as she nervously chewed her nail.

I looked over at Dex and noticed the way he was looking at her, still surprised by the lack of jealousy I felt about it.

"Fuck, Georgia. You're going to be the death of me tonight," I groaned as I slid out from behind her and started undressing.

Dex moved closer, grinning as he lifted the bottom of her shirt and pulled it over her head, revealing she wasn't wearing a bra either. I knew she preferred to go without one when we were at home, but I wasn't sure if she was comfortable enough to do so here. But then again, he had eaten her pussy already, so maybe that comfort threshold had already been crossed.

I stood at the side of the bed, stroking my cock while Dex leaned in and kissed her. She lifted her arms and wrapped her hands behind his neck as her breasts hung heavily between them.

His palms caressed them before he broke the kiss and lowered his mouth to pull a pebbled nipple between his teeth.

"Ahhh," she cried out, letting her head fall back as I crawled onto the bed behind her and wrapped my arms around her stomach. "I need more."

"We got you, baby," I assured her as Dex pulled away and hopped off the bed.

He reached behind and grabbed the top of his shirt, pulling it over his head before tossing it to the floor.

"On your knees, baby," I said, slapping her ass, knowing her pussy was already ready for me.

She grinned and did as I asked, spreading her legs to let me see her glistening arousal. I slid my finger through her part, loving the way her back immediately arched into my touch.

Just as I was about to line my cock up at her entrance, I had another thought.

"You know what, I'm going to have Dex fuck you instead."

Her head whipped up to look at me before she cast a glance at Dex.

"If that's fine with both of you," I added quickly.

I didn't want to be the one to decide when they were ready to cross that line, but I knew that they were both also waiting to see how I felt about it. The least I could do was throw it out there and see how they reacted.

"That's more than fine with me," Georgia said softly.

Dex nodded his head and rubbed his lips together as something weighed on his mind.

"What's wrong?" I asked, unsure whether we should have the conversation in private as best friends or if he was comfortable talking in front of Georgia, given what we were considering doing.

"I don't have a condom."

Shit. I hadn't thought about that. None of us had because none of us came up here with the intention of my best friend fucking my wife.

"I don't either," I said, chewing the side of my lip.

"I'm on birth control," Georgia offered as she looked between us, her ass still on display as she waited on her knees.

"I get tested annually," Dex replied, looking directly at her. "My last check-up was a few months ago. I haven't been with anyone since Andrea."

We all knew about Andrea and how quickly that relationship had ended almost six months ago. While I was surprised he hadn't been with anyone else, I wasn't surprised that I wasn't aware of it, given that Dex had never been one to kiss and tell.

"Okay. I'm fine with that," Georgia said, glancing at me.

"Same." I nodded my head.

"Cool." Dex bobbed his head as he looked around, clearly unsure of what to do now.

"Hey, Dex?"

"Yeah?"

"Do you think you could eat my wife's pussy and make her come before you fuck her senseless?"

I could feel the weight of the tension in the air start to evaporate as Dex grinned and raised an eyebrow at Georgia.

"I would love to."

Seventeen

Dex

I slid my tongue between Georgia's lips, loving how she tasted. I was worried that things might get weird between us, but thankfully, Alex had quickly shifted gears and got us back on track. Georgia was lying on her back, spread wide as I devoured her pussy.

"Fuck. Fuck. Fuck!" she panted as I felt her spasm against my lips, sucking her clit harder as she spiraled over the edge.

My dick ached with need again, already ready after releasing a full load down her throat not that long ago. Now I understood why Alex sometimes had to cancel weekend plans—who could get enough of Georgia? I was on a mission to see how many times we could make her come tonight because I loved the way she looked when she did. I wanted her spent and beyond satisfied by the time we were done with her.

I pulled away and wiped the corners of my mouth as I climbed out from between her legs.

"I'm gonna need a minute," she said with a soft laugh.

"Take all the time you need," I answered, stroking my cock as I stared at her naked body lying on the bed.

Alex sat on the other side of the bed, doing the same.

"I don't know if I can handle all of this cock this weekend," she teased as she sat up.

"Who said it's just this weekend?" Alex pressed, pinning her with a look.

"Well, I guess I just assumed."

"We are stuck here for a few weeks—at minimum," I added.

"Then I guess it looks like we're going to be doing a lot of fucking," she replied with a giggle as she lined herself up in front of me. "How do you want me?"

"I think I want you on your knees with your ass up," I said, remembering how hot she looked earlier when Alex asked her to get in that position.

"You're as bad as Alex, always obsessed with my ass."

"That's because it's fucking hot," I replied, slapping it as she got herself situated.

"Wait until you fuck it," Alex said with a sigh. "Pure heaven."

"I can't wait." I climbed off the bed and stood at the edge, gently guiding her to where I wanted her. "Are you ready?"

"Yes. I've been ready."

I wanted to come just from hearing her say that. My cock twitched in my hand as I lined it up at her entrance and slowly pushed inside. I knew she was used to Alex, and he wasn't small by any means, but I didn't want to assume she would automatically adjust to my size and hurt her.

Her head fell forward as I pushed in deeper, her back arching as she moved her legs slightly to allow me in. I gripped her hips and held tightly as I gave her a few seconds to adjust.

Before I could do anything, she began grinding against me, forcing me to fuck her how she wanted to be fucked. Alex continued stroking his cock as he watched us, but I didn't see any sign of anger on his face.

"I want to suck that," she said to him, nodding to his cock. "Now."

My eyes rolled back in my head as I tried to focus on anything other than coming right then. Her pussy felt incredible as she gripped me tightly and met me thrust for thrust. Alex sat up and crossed the short distance until he was lined up on his knees in front of her. Watching as she took his cock into her mouth was almost my undoing.

I slowed my thrusts so she could suck him without accidentally shoving it all the way down her throat by accident. Alex slid his fingers into her hair and pulled slightly, lifting her head so she could look at him with his cock still in her mouth.

"You look beautiful taking two cocks, Georgia," he murmured, stroking his thumb down her cheek. "Such a good girl."

I felt her pussy tighten around me and knew she needed to come again. I looked up at Alex and smiled when he gave me a nod, letting me know it was okay to fuck her the way she needed to be fucked.

I gripped her hips tightly and thrust hard, pulling out before slamming back inside of her. She cried out, the sound muffled by his cock. I reached a hand down and began rubbing her clit with my finger as I held onto her with my other hand and fucked her hard.

Alex's cock popped out of her mouth, but he just leaned back and continued to stroke it as I fucked her hard and deep. I could feel her tighten around me as I continued working her clit, feeling the moment her orgasm ripped through her.

"Shit!" she cried out as her pussy spasmed around me and a rush of fluid came out.

Alex stroked harder, moving back to give her space as he came on his stomach right at the moment I released my load inside of Georgia. I closed my eyes and gripped her hips harder as I felt the last of it ripple through me. I had never in my life come as hard as I just did with my best friend's wife.

I slowly pulled out, a smug grin pulling at my cheeks knowing how full her pussy was with my cum. In a few minutes, she would have it running down her thighs if we didn't get her cleaned up.

Georgia looked over her shoulder and lifted her head as she kissed me gently before turning her attention back to Alex.

"That was supposed to be for me," she said with a seductive tone to her voice as she crawled the short distance to where he was still sitting on his knees.

I watched as she locked eyes with him as she leaned forward and slowly ran her tongue up his stomach and chest, licking up the cum. He looked down adoringly at his wife as he gripped the back of her head in his hand and caressed it.

I was doing fine until the second I noticed my cum dripping down Georgia's thighs and instantly got hard again. She was, in fact, going to be the death of me.

Eighteen

Georgia

I fucked my husband's best friend.

The thought that Dex had not only eaten my pussy but had fucked me so good I could still feel his dick inside of me was hard to process. I had wanted this for so long, but now that I had it, I couldn't help but worry that it might end as quickly as it started. Just because this was my fantasy didn't mean that it was theirs.

While we all discussed beforehand that we wouldn't let this ruin our friendship, there was no telling what might happen now that the line had fully been crossed. It wasn't even just a little bit crossed—we had full-on jumped over the line, passed Go, collected our two hundred dollars, and were all recovering from marathon-level orgasms.

"Tell me what you're thinking," Alex coaxed as I lay my head against his chest while his finger softly stroked my bare thigh.

"I'm not thinking anything," I said, knowing they were both going to call me on my lie again. And to be honest, I had promised them that I would talk to both of them if anything were bothering me. I didn't want to start whatever this was between the three of us with lies.

"Okay," I rushed out, forcing myself to open up and talk to them. "Now that we've crossed all these lines, I'm worried that things are going to get weird and that everything will end as quickly as it started."

I let out a heavy breath and stared at the TV, avoiding their eyes.

Dex grabbed the remote and turned it off, making a point that I was getting their full attention whether I wanted it or not.

I was sandwiched between them on the bed, so it wasn't like I could go hide in a corner or anything. Now that all of the attention was on me, I questioned whether speaking up was the right move.

"Did you enjoy what we did?" Dex asked softly, his hand resting on mine to get my attention.

I nodded but kept my head forward as I swallowed hard. The heat from his gaze was enough to set my body on fire.

I knew both of them well enough to know they were having some silent discussion between the two of them based on the energy around us. I pulled away from Alex and tried to sit up straight with my knees pulled to my chest as if that would somehow protect my heart.

"Georgia," Dex said, my name sounding different on his lips than before. It was like it was now laced with a different kind of love, one that made my heart ache.

"Hmm?" I pressed my lips together and kept my laser focus on the wall in front of me.

His fingers gently caressed the side of my face as he turned my head to face him. I looked into honey-colored eyes and felt myself getting lost in them.

"Did you enjoy me fucking you?"

I nodded, trying desperately to pull away so I could run and hide somewhere. I didn't care that the rest of the cabin still had no heat. I just needed to get away.

"Did you enjoy me eating your pussy?" he pressed, saying the words as if he were talking about something as simple as the weather as his hand held me in place.

I wanted to answer, but a soft moan escaped my lips instead.

"Good. Because I also enjoyed doing those things with you, Georgia. Just as much as I enjoyed you sucking my cock. I'm okay with all of this, and I don't plan to stop anytime soon."

"I'm also okay with everything that happened," Alex said, pulling my attention to my husband. "It was so fucking hot watching Dex fuck you that I had no choice but to come on myself, Georgia. I'm not bothered that we crossed that line. I would be more bothered if we didn't cross it again because I cannot get enough of you fucking my best friend. But the more important question we need to be asking is how do *you* feel about everything that happened?"

"I agree, I need to know how you're feeling, Georgia. If this isn't what you wanted, then we need to stop right now. Things can go back to how they were before. I'll sleep in the living room—I don't care. I just want to make sure you are okay," Dex added.

I took a deep breath, allowing my shoulders to fall as I exhaled.

"I enjoyed all of it. Way more than I imagined I would. At first, I was nervous about having Dex fuck me while you watched, but then I saw how turned on you were, and that turned me on even more. It was like we were all feeding off of each other's energy and now I can't stop thinking about what it'll be like the next time we… do *something*." I let out a heavy breath, already feeling the weight lift from my shoulders from the worries I was carrying.

"Good. Now let's try to get some rest because we have a long, hard day ahead of us tomorrow," Alex said.

"Like as in marathon sex all day?" I asked, chewing my bottom lip.

"No, as in Dex and I have some work to get started to see if we can get the heater working since we're gonna be up here a while. But I like where your mind is at."

My husband wiggled his eyebrows as I shook my head, fighting a smile. I loved that not only did *he* have a way of calming me, but so did Dex. Not only did I feel better about what happened between us, but I felt the safest and most comfortable with them that I had ever felt before.

Nineteen

Alex

I stood in the kitchen working on breakfast while Georgia slept and Dex took a shower. The news was on, but it did nothing to distract me from thoughts of last night.

The idea of watching Georgia with another man had always turned me on, which was probably why it was always our go-to fantasy that we constantly talked about when we had sex. But actually getting to see it happen was more than I could have ever expected.

I hadn't been jealous one single bit when I saw them together. If anything, it only turned me on more. I thought I had mastered the art of controlling myself, but last night had proved me wrong when I came on my stomach just from the sight of Dex fucking my wife and making her come on his dick.

I flipped the pancakes on the griddle and turned my attention back to the TV as a woman stood outside, bundled up in what appeared to be three winter jackets as she shivered while trying to talk about the storm that had rolled in. The road up the mountain had been closed for the foreseeable future, which meant we were guaranteed to be stuck up here longer than I thought.

Dex came into the living room, which was attached to the kitchen, and gave me a nod in greeting. His attention fell to the story on the TV as he picked up the remote and turned the volume up. We both listened as she talked about the four to six inches of snow we were expected to get tonight, in addition to what had already fallen since the storm first rolled in.

I put the last few pancakes on a plate and turned off the stove right as Georgia came in. Her hair was pulled into a lopsided bun on the top of her head as she wrapped her arms around herself to keep warm.

"Good morning," I said, leaning in to kiss her as she walked over to me.

"Good morning. Was the news just saying we're supposed to get *more* snow?" she asked as she looked between Dex and me.

"Yeah. Not a ton, maybe four to six inches."

She raised her eyebrows and stared at me.

"Maybe we should define your idea of a ton, because four to six inches is a lot," Georgia objected as she pulled a chair out and sat at the kitchen table.

I grabbed the food and set it in front of her, then grabbed plates for everyone.

"Yeah, but you easily took ten inches last night," Dex said to her with a grin as he pulled out a chair and sat beside her.

Her cheeks flushed the prettiest shade of pink as she pressed her lips together and tried not to smile.

"And if you look at how much dick you took altogether last night, it's at least twenty inches. Give or take," I added, joining them.

"You guys are the worst," Georgia muttered, shaking her head as she continued to struggle not to smile.

"I don't know, baby. The way you came last night says otherwise," I purred in her ear as she reached for a pancake and added it to her plate.

"So, what is the plan for today?" she asked, effectively changing the subject.

"After breakfast, I'm going to take a look at the heater and see if I can get that running. I'm also going to clear out the fireplace in here so if we can't get the heater working, we can at least keep this room warm."

"I can work on the fireplace if you want," Dex offered, knowing there wasn't much space for both of us to work on the heater.

"Sure. That sounds great. Thanks."

"What am I supposed to do?" Georgia asked, looking between us.

"Rest," we both said at the same time.

Obviously, great minds thought alike.

"Why do I need to rest?"

"Because we have wicked plans for you later," I replied, wiggling my eyebrows as she rolled her eyes.

****

I grinned as I stood there with my hands up to the vents, feeling the warm air blowing out. It had taken longer than I expected to fix the heater, but I was thrilled that it was finally working. This would cut down on how much firewood we were going through unless the power went out. With the storm being as bad as it was, I didn't want to have to worry about running out of firewood and not being able to get more for a while.

"Oh my gosh! It's working!" Georgia squealed as she came rushing over to me as I stood at the end of the hallway. "How did you fix it?"

"Well, it turned out that it just needed to be cleaned. God knows when the last time was that any maintenance was done on it. I found a pack of new filters in the hallway closet, and I'm guessing they're the same ones I bought a few years ago that my grandmother promised she would get someone to change for her."

"Poor thing. She really wanted to take care of this place," Georgia replied, her voice filled with emotion for my grandmother.

"I know. It breaks my heart that she can't come up here to enjoy it anymore. But at the same time, I'm glad that it's us who are stuck up here instead of her."

We walked back into the living room, where Dex was finishing up with the fireplace.

"I think we are good to go," he said, standing up and wiping his hands on the front of his jeans.

"Thanks for getting it cleaned out. I got the heater working, but it will be nice to have the fireplace ready in case we need to use it when the power goes out," I replied.

"You think we'll lose power?" Georgia asked with concern etched on her face.

"It's always a possibility."

"What will we do if it does?"

"I don't know," I said with a shrug. "Fuck nonstop to stay warm?"

"That's not funny," she teased as she smacked my chest. "I'm being serious. Do we have everything we need if the power goes out?"

"Yeah, baby. We'll be just fine. Dex and I stocked up on flashlights and batteries when we were at the store. I'll make sure to leave a flashlight in here and one in our bedroom. We have two working fireplaces now, so we can keep the house warm, and we bought plenty of food to last us several weeks."

"What if the fireplace in here doesn't work?" Georgia asked, chewing her nail as she stared at it.

"We still have the one in the bedroom," I responded, noticing something was bothering her.

"Oh. Okay."

"What's wrong?" Dex asked, standing on the other side of her, noticing the same thing I was.

"Nothing," she lied, her voice rising slightly.

"Georgia…" I warned.

"Fine," she groaned and tipped her head back as she closed her eyes. "While I love the giant bed that we can mess around in, I'm feeling a little stir crazy being cooped up in the bedroom. There's no window to look out of. It's dark in there. I feel a little like I'm going to go crazy if we have to spend all of our time in there."

I nodded my head, finally understanding. Georgia loved being able to look outside, which was why we had large windows throughout our house in the city. The natural light always lifted her mood, so I could only imagine how off and down she had been feeling, not being able to do any of that. We had spent time in the living room decorating the house yesterday, but it was short-lived due to how cold it was. I knew I should have taken the time to inspect the heater instead of worrying about decorating, but I wanted to do something that would make her happy.

"Dex can try to start a fire in it while we have power to make sure it works. I'm sorry that we've been so cooped up in the bedroom. I should have made fixing the heater my top priority. I'm so sorry, baby," I said as I placed my hands on her hips and held her.

"It's not a big deal. I thought I was going to be fine with it, but this morning I woke up and it was so dark in the room. It just really messed with my head. Then I heard the news about more snow coming, and it just totally shifted my mood."

"It's understandable," Dex said as he grabbed a few pieces of wood for the fire. "I don't think I could spend all day and night cooped up in that room either. But the nice thing is that I'm pretty sure I got this one up and running, so even if the power goes out and we lose the heater, we should be good to hang out in here. Should we check it and see?"

I nodded, pulling Georgia against my chest as I held her from behind. We watched as Dex set the wood in the fireplace and struck a match, holding the flame to the wood while we waited to see if it would work. Within a few seconds, the kindling was burning, creating a new warmth around us as the smoke floated up and out of the chimney.

"There we go," Dex said, stepping back and smiling at his work. "We're good to go. Even if we lose power, we can use the fireplace in here."

"Thank you. I'm sorry to be such a pain."

"You're not a pain at all. We want you to be comfortable, especially since we're going to be here for a while."

"I hate to ask," Georgia said, lifting her hands in front of her as if begging.

"You can ask for anything, baby. What does my beautiful wife want?"

"Do you mind if I start cleaning the cabin? It is driving me *nuts*."

I let my head drop forward as I shook it while the grin spread across my face. She was so fucking cute.

"Yes, Georgia. You can clean," I replied with a chuckle. While I didn't want to keep her from doing something that would make her feel better, I also didn't bring her up to the cabin so she could clean. I wanted her to relax instead—or better yet—I wanted to forget all of the things we needed to get done and spend my time worshipping her body and the things I could do to it.

"Eeek! Thank you, baby! I promise I won't get in the way. I know you guys have work to do around here, so I can clean the rooms you won't be in."

"And here I thought you were going to ask for a sexual favor or something," I replied sarcastically.

"Well, I would, but I'm saving those for later." She winked and pulled out of my arms as she grinned over her shoulder while running to the kitchen to gather the supplies she needed.

One thing about Georgia was that clean, bright rooms bursting with sunshine filled her up better than Dex or I ever could.

Twenty

Dex

Seeing the smile on Georgia's face as she sat on the couch and stared out the window made my heart swell. She had already cleaned the entire kitchen and living room while Alex and I worked on fixing the hole in the wall. It was unknown why the hole existed in the first place, but since we had the necessary materials to fix it, we patched it up and considered the job done.

"Did you want to watch a movie?" Alex asked her as he walked by and noticed the TV wasn't turned on.

Georgia shook her head and lifted her cup of tea to her lips, smiling as she watched the snow fall outside. We had gone through and opened all of the blinds now that the heater was working and we didn't need to try to conserve energy. It felt nice to have the light in the room, and even I felt my spirits lifting—not that I had been depressed about being trapped in the cabin with a beautiful woman who was obsessed with my cock.

Alex leaned down and kissed the top of her head before heading to the kitchen. The remodeling that had been started before we got here was more or less complete, minus a few finishing touches. Like the cabinets had already been installed and painted, but none of the doors were attached. Alex mentioned seeing some in the guest room earlier, so it was on our list to get them hung tomorrow. I hated that we didn't have all of the supplies we needed to get everything done, but it was nice that we could work on some of it. Progress was progress, even when it was small. Plus, it wasn't like we were leaving any time soon, which gave us all the time in the world to get things done.

"Do you want steak or chicken for dinner?" Alex asked as he stared into the fridge and leaned against the door.

"What does Georgia want?"

"I don't think we're going to get much out of her until the sun goes down," he replied, looking over his shoulder.

"She really does love watching the snow fall."

He nodded as we both looked longingly at his wife.

"I think she just likes feeling like she's not trapped in here. Watching the snow fall is more peaceful for her now that we have the heater up and running and don't have to keep the blinds closed to try to conserve heat. I think that's what was really bothering her."

"Well, at least we're getting some stuff done. That feels good."

"Yeah. I wish we had what we needed, but then again, I should have known the weather would be bad and planned ahead. It's not like I didn't spend most of my childhood coming up here to celebrate the holidays with my grandparents. I knew how bad these storms could get. I should have purchased what we needed in town before we came up."

"Even then, it was hard to know what we would need until we got here. You said yourself that your grandmother couldn't remember what had been finished and what still needed to be done."

"I'm just glad that we're getting things working around here. Between the heater and the fireplace in here, that gives me peace of mind if the power goes out."

"I honestly can't believe how much Georgia cleaned. It looks like a completely different cabin," I acknowledged, looking around.

"She loves to clean. It calms her."

"I can see that." I laughed as I looked over at her, fully relaxed on the couch as if she didn't have a care in the world.

"Alright. How about steak for dinner? I can get started on the baked potatoes since they'll need longer to cook."

"That works for me. Let me know what you need help with."

"I got it. If you want to go keep Georgia company, that works for me."

I nodded, noticing that the Christmas tree hadn't been plugged in yet. We had moved it out of the way when we fixed the wall, but forgot to plug it in. I felt Georgia's eyes on me as the tree lit up, casting a warm glow in the corner of the room with the soft white lights sparkling on it.

"Thank you," she said softly, pulling her feet in and tucking them beneath her to make room for me on the couch. I knew it had looked a little worn down when I first saw it, but it was surprisingly comfortable, and the blanket Georgia had put over it was super soft.

"No problem." I smiled and gave her leg a quick squeeze before leaning forward to grab the remote from the coffee table. I noticed a book sitting beside it with a man on the cover. He didn't have a head, just a shirtless man with ripped abs lying on the bed. I picked it up and studied it, feeling the heat from her gaze.

I looked over at her and arched an eyebrow. Her cheeks flushed as she lifted her cup to her lips and tried to hide behind it.

"Third Time's The Charm," I read out loud, noticing the way she squirmed as I flipped it over and read the back. "Let me guess, it takes him three times before he can find her clit?"

She shook her head, her grin as cute as her blush.

"Capshaw doesn't need any help finding her clit," she replied, her voice still quiet.

"Is that so?"

She nodded, lowering her cup slightly.

"Does it take him three times of trying to fuck her before she lets him?"

She giggled and shook her head.

"Capshaw doesn't have any trouble getting women to want to go to bed with him."

I furrowed my brow and flipped it back to the front so I could see this man better.

"Should I be jealous of this guy?" I asked, only somewhat kidding.

She shrugged and pressed her lips together.

"Fuck. I guess I need to buy you a new book when we go to the store again."

"You will have to try to pry that book out of my cold, dead hands," she warned as she set the cup down on the coffee table.

I flipped through the pages, noticing several corners that were folded over. My eyes widened in horror as I opened the book to the last one I found. I turned it to her and pointed at the bent corner.

"You are a monster," I shrieked playfully, clutching my other hand to my heart to drive home how much this hurt me. "What kind of person folds the page, Georgia?"

She threw her hands up and stared at me.

"I didn't bring a bookmark with me."

"This is a crime. Book lovers across the world are feeling their hearts break over the damage you've done to these pages," I teased, scanning the words on the page when a few caught my eye. My eyebrows rose high on my forehead, and I could feel the heat as it flushed over my face. I looked at Georgia and lowered the book as she lifted her hands and tried to hide from me.

"My, my, my. This is quite the dirty book you're reading."

She squirmed, trying to pull away from me as I grabbed her thigh and held her steady. I propped the book open with one hand, using my fingers to keep it open as I read the filthy words on page 112.

"Fucking you so good you won't be able to walk right for days. Is that what you want, Kensy?" I looked at Georgia and found her blush trailing down over her chest as she continued to hide from me. I read quickly, already so captivated by this book that I wasn't sure I was going to give it back to her. *"He moved beside me and licked his lips, showing me the evidence of my arousal on his face before casually wiping it away with his hand. You taste just like I thought you would, he said quietly, brushing a strand of hair out of my face."*

I could feel my cock hardening as I continued reading, not sure who I was reading aloud for at this point—me or Georgia.

"Mmm hmm. And I lied earlier. Those were the second-best tacos I've ever had. This is now officially the best, he teased as his hand reached down and caressed my overly sensitive pussy."

I took a deep breath and closed the book, letting my hand trail up Georgia's thigh as she let her leg fall to the side for me.

Fuck.

"I changed my mind on dinner," I called to Alex, making sure he could hear me.

"Yeah? What do you want instead?" he asked.

Thankfully, he hadn't done much aside from turning the oven on and gathering the potatoes to wash.

"Tacos."

Twenty-One

Georgia

Hearing Dex read me the book had been my undoing. I knew it was spicy, but hearing a man who had been between my legs several times already say those filthy things had me wet and aching for his cock.

"I can make tacos," Alex confirmed, completely unaware of why Dex suddenly asked for them. Or at least I assumed he was clueless about the context. It wasn't like it was a big room with background noise to drown us out. It wouldn't surprise me if Alex had heard what Dex had been reading and was ready to make me squirm with desire as much as Dex was.

Dex set the book back down on the coffee table, closer to him than where I had originally put it.

"Are you stealing my book?" I asked, lifting an eyebrow.

"Yes. I need it for research."

"I highly doubt that," I replied with a laugh.

"Nope. It's true. The guy in this book makes you squirm and blush just by mentioning his name; therefore, I need to see what it is he's doing that we need to do."

"It's just a book. He's literally a figment of the author's imagination."

"Have you masturbated to the book?"

"No," I rushed out, my cheeks flaming with heat again. At this point, I was going to have to ask them to turn down the heater and put out the fire that was roaring across from us. I didn't want to get into any details about if or when I touched myself, but I could tell by the look on his face that Dex wasn't going to let this go.

"No? So is this the first spicy part in the book?" he asked, his brow furrowed as he thought through whatever his mind was focused on.

I nodded, not willing to say anymore.

He took a deep breath and let it out slowly as his hand slid up my thigh, getting painfully close to my pussy. Suddenly, I wished I hadn't put the fleece-lined leggings on because it was getting too hot for them.

"Have you masturbated to other books?" he pressed, something changing in his tone.

My eyes widened as embarrassment washed over me.

"I thought so. I want a full list of your favorite books."

"Dex, you can't be serious," I replied with a laugh.

"I am. I want to know what happens in these books that makes you touch yourself, Georgia. If anything, I think it's pretty clear now that Alex and I are willing to do whatever it takes to make your fantasies come true. I have nothing against these books and want you to keep reading them. I just want to read them too, so I can see what it is that you want. What you like."

"I have her purchase history on my Amazon account," Alex offered. "We can look at them later. I know she brought a handful of books with her for the trip up here, so we can also start there."

So he was listening.

"Perfect. We can check them out later and see where we want to start," Dex said, brushing his hand against my pussy.

I closed my eyes and hissed, frustrated when he pulled away.

He got up and grabbed the book, taking it with him as he went to the kitchen table and sat down.

I wasn't sure what I was more mad about—that he had stolen my book or that he left me wet and aching for a release.

Twenty-Two

Alex

I couldn't help but watch Georgia as she stared at Dex's mouth as it parted to take a bite of his taco. She licked her lips, so completely transfixed on his every movement that she hadn't even noticed my hand as it slid up her thigh until I gripped it tightly.

Her head whipped toward me, eyes wide with surprise when she realized she had been caught.

"You okay?" I asked, keeping my voice low as she melted into my touch.

Dex lifted his eyes to look at us, but kept eating.

She nodded, offering me a slight smile, and then looked away.

"Just making sure since you've hardly eaten anything. I mean, I get that you don't love *tacos* as much as Dex does, but I want to make sure you eat."

"I love eating tacos," Dex replied, swiping his tongue over his lip to catch any crumbs. Or more so because he knew

Georgia was watching and wanted to torture my horny wife.

The blush on her cheeks deepened as she looked away from him and studied her plate.

Dex finished his food and wiped his mouth before getting up from the table and clearing his plate.

"I'm going to go take a shower," he said nonchalantly.

I knew he was really just giving Georgia some space since she seemed more flustered than normal. I nodded, thankful that he could read her as well as I could.

Once he was out of the room, I squeezed her thigh and waited for her to look at me.

"What's wrong, baby?"

"Nothing," she replied with a heavy sigh that didn't feel like *nothing*.

"If things are getting to be too much with Dex, I can talk to him and as—"

"I'm horny," she whispered harshly, looking over her shoulder to make sure he wasn't there to hear. "I'm so fucking horny that I can't eat because I watch Dex eat those fucking tacos and remember how he felt when he ate *my taco*. And now I can't think about anything else, and I'm uncomfortable and hungry—"

"Okay, okay," I rushed out with a soft laugh as I held my hands up to stop her. "I know how to fix this."

She tilted her head and arched an eyebrow at me.

"Stand up," I said, scooting back from the table so I could help take her leggings off.

She eyed me cautiously as I pulled the fabric down her legs and tossed it behind me. Just the sight of her in that lace thong was enough to get me hard immediately. I unbuckled my jeans and lowered the zipper before pulling my cock out and stroking it.

Georgia's eyes lit up as she started to bend down before I stopped her. She frowned with disappointment when I shook my head.

"Sit on my cock, Georgia," I commanded, spreading my legs and adjusting to give her room. "Sit on my cock and face the table."

Nervously, she climbed over me, hovering above my cock as I felt the warmth of her pussy. I gently rubbed a finger along her slit, cursing when I felt how wet she was. I pulled her thong to the side and held my dick as I helped guide it inside of her. Once she was situated, I thrust my hips upward, making sure I was as deep as she could take me.

She whimpered as her head fell back and she rocked her hips.

I reached over and grabbed her plate of food, setting it in front of her.

"Eat," I said, my voice gruff as I tried not to come undone right away. It had been days since I'd fucked her, and I had forgotten how magical her pussy was.

"Alex, you can't be serious," she said, looking over her shoulder at me.

I grabbed her t-shirt and bunched it in my fist, lifting it so I could hold onto her hips as I thrust up into her again.

"I'm dead serious. Start eating, or I'm not going to fuck you."

"Are you threatening me?"

"I am. With a good time. Now stop talking and eat, Georgia."

She giggled and lifted the taco to her mouth, taking a bite as I started thrusting the best I could in this position. I heard her moan, but kept going, knowing that I would have to hold off until she finished eating before I could finish her the way I wanted to.

Georgia kept eating, her body tensing every time I would go harder. She finished one taco and started on another when she decided to close her legs enough that she could brace her feet on the floor. She cupped the bottom of the taco with one hand while she ate it, bouncing as hard as she could on my cock.

"Fuck, Georgia," I warned, gripping her hips tighter to try to keep from coming. "Baby…"

"I want you to come," she whispered in between bites.

Taco meat fell all over the table and floor around us, but I didn't care. I would make Georgia another dinner after we were finished if I had to. Right now, the only thing I cared about was my smoking hot wife riding my dick while devouring her tacos. She leaned back against my chest, slowing herself slightly as I reached forward and started rubbing her clit.

The taco fell from her hand and onto her plate as she leaned against me and allowed herself to fall over the edge. Her pussy spasmed against my finger while sucking every last ounce of my cum out as I came deep inside of her.

We were both panting as she rested against my chest and tried to catch her breath.

"Now, do you think you can finish eating? You're going to need that energy," I whispered playfully in her ear.

A few minutes later, she climbed off me and grabbed her leggings as I cleaned myself off and tucked my dick back into my jeans. I knew it wouldn't be long before I fucked Georgia again, and that made me smile.

After she finished eating, I worked on clearing our plates and loaded the dishwasher while Georgia went to the bathroom to clean up. A few minutes later, Dex came in and grinned when he saw the mess on the floor. He folded his arms over his chest and leaned against the door frame, studying me as I grabbed the broom and swept it up.

"What happened in here?" he asked coyly, the corners of his lips turning up into a smirk.

"Nothing," I lied, knowing he already knew. "Just wanted to make sure Georgia got enough to eat since she was so distracted by you eating tacos."

He lowered his head and tried to hide his smile that was now fully plastered across his face.

"I would say sorry, but I'm not. I like that she responds so easily to me," he admitted.

"I like it too. Even if I have to fuck her while she eats because she's too wound up to focus on feeding herself."

"Fuck. I would have loved to watch that."

"Well, maybe I'll make tacos every night," I teased, pressing my tongue against the roof of my mouth as Georgia returned and studied us.

"And why will you be making tacos every night?" she asked, folding her arms over her chest to mimic Dex.

 I stepped closer to her, letting the broom lean against the table as I wrapped my arm around her waist and pulled her into me.

"Because I love how fucking horny you get when you watch him eat tacos, and I can't get enough of it."

She looked up at me from beneath dark lashes, and a devious smile spread across her cheeks.

"I like it when he eats in general. Tacos. Sandwiches. My pussy," she said, whispering the last word.

"Fuck," Dex muttered, lowering his head but not saying anything else.

"What's wrong? Cat got your tongue?" Georgia asked, her bratty side starting to show.

I felt my dick harden again, knowing she would continue acting out until she got fucked the way she wanted to be fucked. Our little quickie at the dinner table was just an appetizer to hold her over until we could quell the ache together.

Dex pushed off the wall and crossed the short space between us as he stared down at her, desire flooding his eyes.

"Be careful with that mouth of yours, Georgia," he warned, though I could tell he was as turned on by it as I was.

"Or what?" she pressed, tilting her chin up in defiance.

He pinched it between his fingers and lowered her head as he licked his lips and stared at her.

"Be careful, or you'll be choking on my cock as I shove it down your throat again."

She let out an audible gasp as he gave her one last look then pulled away and grabbed a bottle of water from the fridge. He opened the cap, tipped his head back, and chugged.

I watched as Georgia studied him again, noticing the way his throat bobbed as he drank the entire bottle without taking a break. He tossed it in the trash and then walked past us, stopping to look Georgia up and down in a way that I knew had her toes curling.

"Better hydrate, Georgia. You're going to need all of your energy for what I have in store for you."

He winked and walked out of the room as she turned to putty in my arms. I chuckled and held her, knowing that Dex wasn't just playing anymore. Georgia unlocked something inside of him that would make him feral, and he would go to any length necessary to show her just how much she belonged to him now.

Twenty-Three

Dex

I tried to ignore the way my body desperately craved Georgia as she sat on the couch between me and Alex and read her book. We had compromised that I would let her finish the one she was already reading before I officially stole it. But it was killing me not knowing what she was reading that was making her blush as she tried to hide her smile.

"What page are you on?" I asked, nudging her knee with mine to get her attention.

"One fifty-two," she replied, her body flushed with color.

"What's happening?" I pressed, leaning closer to try to look over her shoulder.

She chewed her lower lip and turned the book to face me so I could read it.

"Secrets don't make friends," Alex teased, nodding for me to read it out loud.

I cleared my throat, trying to find a good place to start when my mind was racing for me to keep reading.

"I took a deep breath and tried to get used to the cold. His fingers continued to tickle my skin as he moved the ice cube around, then I felt him part my folds and slip the ice cube inside. I bolted forward, only to be greeted by his other hand gently pushing me back onto the bed. "Trust me," he instructed before lowering his mouth to my pussy, the warmth of his breath creating a new sensation against the cold sting of the ice cube." My cock was hard as a rock as I finished reading it.

"Fuck," Alex said as he pushed out a heavy breath. "That was fucking hot. Do you want to try that, Georgia?"

"Wait, it gets better," I said, holding up my hand to interrupt them. "He fucks her with a cucumber too."

I lowered the book and looked at both of them. Alex looked like he was trying to hold himself together while Georgia blushed seven shades of red.

"It's just fiction," Georgia rushed out, lowering her head as she took the book from me.

"And?" Alex pressed softly. "What does that mean?"

"I don't know. That it's just made-up stuff that someone thought of and put in a book. It doesn't mean this happens in real life."

"Baby, I've used ice on you several times. It's not just made-up stuff." Alex lifted his eyebrows at her.

"Yeah, but you never stuck it inside of me," she countered. "Nor have you fucked me with a cucumber."

"We can remedy that," I offered, way too enthusiastic about the thought of trying new things with Georgia.

"I'm not letting either of you fuck me with a cucumber. Thanks, but no thanks."

"Okay, then how about the ice. The thought of it obviously turned you on," Alex said.

"No, it didn't," she objected with a weird laugh. "I'm just *shocked* for Kensy. That's all."

"Because Capshaw can do no wrong?" I offered, knowing I would get her to confess how extremely turned on she was right now. Alex and I could both see it, even if she was denying it.

"It's fiction," she objected, letting the book close as she held it on her lap.

"Okay, then if I stuck my hand in your panties right now, they wouldn't be wet?" I purposely let my voice drop to the octave that I knew always sent goosebumps over her skin.

"Nope." She let the 'p' pop in a way that told me she was lying.

"You sure about that?" I asked, slowly running my hand up her thigh as she tracked my every movement. She had changed into a pair of cotton shorts that barely covered her ass after she complained about getting too hot on the couch, and I loved the easy access.

Her eyes watched as I slowly inched higher, my fingers brushing against her panties before slightly lifting them enough to slip one finger inside. She inhaled sharply and held her breath as I took my time caressing her with that finger before letting it slide along her seam, feeling how wet she was.

"Fuck, Georgia," I groaned, pulling my finger out and licking it.

I didn't miss the look in Alex's eye as he watched me do it. This was turning him on as much as it was me, and I needed to do something about it.

"Stand up and take your shorts off," I demanded as I stood up, pulled my shirt over my head, and tossed it to the floor.

Her eyebrows rose in disbelief.

"Panties too," I continued, pulling my lower lip between my teeth. "Now, Georgia. Before I lose my patience."

"Are you going to make me?" she asked, that same bratty attitude from earlier reappearing.

"Baby, you don't want me to *make* you do anything," I warned, lifting an eyebrow.

"Hmm… I don't know. That sounds like another failed promise. Just like you swore that if I didn't watch my mouth, your cock would be going down it. Yet here we are." She spread her arms out and stayed put, making my cock twitch with how turned on I was getting.

"You don't know what you just got yourself into," Alex said with a sigh as he leaned back against the couch and watched us.

"I'm not scared," Georgia said, jutting her chin out.

"Good. You should never be *scared* when it comes to me, Georgia."

"See, such big talk and little bite," she started before I bent down and grabbed her, tossing her over my shoulder as the book fell from her lap.

She squealed and swatted at my back as I charged into the bedroom and deposited her on the bed. She sat in the middle of it, watching me as she chewed her nail. I left the room and went to the toolbox in the living room, looking for what I needed.

Alex tipped his head back and laughed, holding a hand to his stomach as he noticed the rope in one hand and the drill in the other. I could hear him following behind me as I went back to the bedroom and smirked at Georgia. Her eyes widened, staring at everything as I laid it on the bed.

Ideally, I would take my time, pull the beds out, and make a plan for what I was doing, but my cock was hard, which made me an impatient bastard. So I climbed onto the bed and tapped the wall several times until I found the stud, then began drilling. I secured the heavy-duty stainless steel pad eye hook before scooting over to the next stud and securing the other.

I stepped back and looked at them, pleased with my work.

"Do I even want to know what you're up to?" Georgia asked, looking up at me.

"Probably not," I admitted as I stared down at her. From this angle, I could see right down her shirt and groaned at the fact that she wasn't wearing a bra.

"You did that quickly," she murmured as I climbed off the bed and set the drill down.

"I am a general contractor, so this is kinda in my wheelhouse."

"You frequently install hooks in the wall above a bed?" she questioned, tilting her head to study me.

"Only at my house." I winked and put everything on the floor out of the way.

"And you just happen to keep those hooks in your toolbox?" she pressed.

"I actually bought them at the store the other day." I shrugged, not bothering to tell her that Alex had another use for them. But by the look on his face, I knew he didn't care what I was using them for tonight.

He leaned against the doorframe and watched us.

"Shirt off," I told her, giving her a nod as I picked up the rope and examined it in my hand. It wasn't what I would typically use, and I didn't want to hurt her. I put it down and made a note to get better supplies for next time.

I pulled the belt through the loops of my jeans and loved the way she watched me as she took off her shirt and tossed it to Alex. He grinned as he caught it.

"Shorts and panties, too," I demanded, my dick already hard and begging to be inside of her again.

She stared at me with a look that told me she was more into this than she was letting on. She held eye contact with me as she slipped both off and threw them to the floor. Seeing her naked and not being able to take her right away was nearly my undoing.

"You've had a smart mouth all night," I said as I slowly climbed onto the bed and prowled toward her. "I think it's time we did something about that."

She giggled and chewed her lip to try to stop herself.

"Arms in front of you," I instructed, holding the belt out as she slowly put them in front of me.

I felt her heated gaze on me as I wrapped the belt several times around her wrists before tying it in a knot. Thankfully, it was rather worn, so it bent easily, but it wouldn't be enough to keep her restrained the way I wanted. I grabbed the rope and looped it through the knot I had made, then pulled it to where I needed it.

"Scoot all the way back against the wall and sit on your knees."

Her face flushed as she followed my command.

Once she was situated, I tied the rope to each of the hooks, pulling on it to make sure it was secure. Her arms pulled tightly above her head as she looked up, trying to see what I had done.

"Is this okay?" I asked, checking to make sure she was okay with being restrained.

She nodded, the heat flushing across her skin.

I leaned in and grabbed the back of her head, holding her still as I pressed my lips to hers, kissing hard. She whimpered and opened her mouth, allowing me access as I pulled away.

"Dex," she whined, batting her eyes as she stared at me, wanting more.

"I already told you about that smart mouth of yours, baby. Now you're going to see just how little mercy I have when you act up."

I licked my lips and then laid down on the bed, scooting myself until my mouth was lined up right below her pussy. Georgia's height gave me an advantage with her being closer to the bed on her knees, which allowed me to eat her pussy without having to pull her down. I gripped her thighs and slowly swiped my tongue along her slit, making her jump as she hissed.

I grinned, knowing she was already fully turned on and ready to come, but I was going to make her wait as long as I could so she knew I wasn't the guy to play with. While I would give Georgia anything she wanted, I also had no problem helping fix her attitude when needed. And by the looks of it, neither did Alex.

Twenty-Four

Georgia

"Fuck," I hissed, letting my head fall back in frustration as Dex brought me to the edge of climax and then suddenly pulled away again. He'd been edging me for at least ten minutes, and I felt like my body was going to explode.

"I warned you," he teased, though I was tempted to put all of my weight on his face and suffocate him at this point.

"You're just being mean," I argued, looking down as his chest shook slightly as he laughed.

"Trust me, you'll come when it's time."

"I am starting to doubt that," I hissed, squirming against his face, desperate for any friction I could get.

Before I could say anything, Dex bit my clit, putting just enough pain there to startle me before he started sucking it. My head fell back as my eyes closed, my body bracing itself for one of the biggest orgasms I was about to have.

I tried not to get my hopes up, knowing how much Dex and Alex were getting off on watching me suffer. I wouldn't put it past Dex to tease me to the point of breaking, just to stop and force my orgasm away again.

My face scrunched as the sensation intensified, the tingling up my spine growing stronger.

I gasped, trying to remember to breathe as I stayed focused on his mouth on my pussy, bringing me such delicious torture. His hands gripped my hips, holding me in place as he mercilessly sucked my clit until the first wave of pleasure rolled over me.

"Ahhh," I cried out, arching my back as I tried to get away from how intense it felt but Dex wouldn't let me. Everything was beyond sensitive as he kept going, not letting up even the slightest.

"I can't," I objected quickly, looking down to see his death grip on my hips. "Dex, I can't. I need a break. It's too much. I'm too sensitive."

"Just try to relax," Alex said softly, stepping further into the room from where he had been watching off to the side. "Slowly breathe through it."

"But I can't. It's too much. I'm overly sen—" My words died on my tongue as I moaned loudly, feeling another orgasm rush through me.

My body went limp, the rope tugging against the hooks as I struggled to stay upright.

"Fuck. What was that?" I asked, panting as Dex slid out from underneath me and licked his lips.

"I'm guessing she's never had multiple orgasms before?" he asked Alex, as if *I* wasn't the one asking the question.

Multiple orgasms? Since when was that something that really happened?

"Nope. I've tried, but she always tenses up. I should have thought of restraining her. That seemed to help," Alex replied, winking at me as Dex worked on untying everything.

He slowly lowered my arms and then removed the belt, rubbing the skin softly as he studied me to make sure I was okay.

"Are you good?" he asked, his voice soft.

I nodded, still too stunned to get words out. How the hell had he done that?

"I think that's the first time I've seen her attitude change so quickly," Alex joked, climbing onto the bed beside us.

I looked at him and rolled my eyes as I grinned and laid down, too exhausted to hold myself up anymore.

"Well, at least we have some ideas of what works," Dex teased, lying on the other side of me.

"There are plenty of things that work," I said, adding to the conversation.

"Oh yeah, like what?" Alex asked, pulling my attention to him.

Being sandwiched between them was my new favorite place to be.

"Umm… Well… Maybe…" I chewed my lip nervously, no longer feeling as brave to get the words out as I had felt a few seconds ago.

"Just spit it out," Dex said with a laugh.

"Georgia doesn't *spit*. She swallows," Alex said, popping up on his elbow to look over at Dex.

"True." Dex nodded his head as if he knew this about me.

"So, what were you thinking, baby?"

I took a slow, deep breath in as I felt my husband's arms wrap around me as he waited for my answer.

"I was thinking that maybe we could try the thing you guys were talking about… You know, where both of you…"

My face was on fire as I struggled to get the words out. If I couldn't even talk about it with them, how in the world was I ever going to *do* it with them?

"You want to get fucked by both of us at the same time?" Alex asked, clarifying what I couldn't say.

I nodded, pressing my lips together to keep from saying anything stupid.

"I can't think of anything I'd like more than that," Alex replied, softly stroking a hand up my arm as chills spread over my skin.

"I haven't been able to stop thinking about it since we mentioned it the other night," Dex admitted. "If you're sure that's what you want to do, I'm in."

"I want to do it," I said with more confidence than ever.

Alex nodded to Dex, some unspoken conversation happening between them that I wasn't made part of. I was about to question what it was, but then Alex wrapped his arm around me and pulled me next to him as he lowered his mouth to mine. My eyes fluttered closed as my body melted into his touch. His tongue swiped across my lip, demanding access as I felt Dex's muscular body slide behind me.

I moaned and parted my lips as I felt the distinct hardness of his erection against my ass while my husband teased my mouth. My body was already on fire with both of their hands roaming over it, caressing me in ways that had my toes curling.

Dex kissed the side of my neck, pushing my hair out of the way as Alex's fingers slid over my pussy, slipping through my arousal. My head tipped back, careful not to hit Dex as he continued kissing his way down my back.

Alex pulled his finger free and sucked it into his mouth, groaning as he did it.

He got up and quickly undressed before lying down on his back and looking at me.

"Come sit on my cock, baby," he said, his voice low.

Dex pulled away, watching as I carefully did as my husband asked. I closed my eyes as I slowly lowered myself onto his dick, taking him inch by inch until he was fully seated inside of me. His hands soothingly slid up and down my thighs, encouraging me to relax as I sat there.

Typically, I would already be bouncing and riding his cock like there was no tomorrow, but I knew what the plan was. I moved my hips slowly, grinding against him while Dex undressed behind us. Alex and I had done anal sex plenty of times before, so I wasn't a stranger to it. But we hadn't done it while someone else's cock was inside of me, so I wasn't sure how this was going to work.

Dex climbed onto the bed behind me, gently caressing my skin with his hands as my back leaned against his chest.

"If at any time you want me to stop, you say so," Dex said firmly.

I nodded, too overwhelmed with emotions to speak. I was equal parts excited as I was nervous, but overall, I was mostly horny, and the thought of being with both of them at the same time had me practically dripping.

"I need to hear you say it."

"I will let both of you know if it gets to be too much and I want to stop," I said, my voice clear and loud enough for them to hear me.

"Good girl," Dex murmured as he wrapped a hand around my waist and gently pulled me against him as I started moving my hips again.

His hands teased my breasts, his fingers stimulating my nipples while Alex gripped my hips and thrust up inside of me. Feeling them like this alone was already overstimulating; I could only imagine how over the edge it would be to have both of their cocks inside of me.

I closed my eyes and focused on Alex as he took over guiding me, pulling me slightly until I was almost lying on his chest. I heard the distinctive sound of the bottle of lube opening before I felt the cold liquid on my skin as Dex's fingers worked to spread it generously where I would need it.

While Alex kissed me, Dex worked a finger inside of my ass before inserting another. I let out a soft moan from the sensation as shivers spread over my skin. Slowly, he moved them around, working me so I could take his cock next.

"Are you ready?" Dex asked, his voice hoarse as he gently pulled his fingers out.

I nodded.

"Yes," I breathed out, trying not to tense up.

Alex pulled me closer to him, forcing my body to cover his in a way that kept his cock inside of me and gave Dex better access to my ass. I felt Dex's hands as they gripped my hips to hold me steady before he slowly pushed the head of his cock inside.

I hissed and tipped my head back as I exhaled heavily, everyone completely still while I got used to the feeling.

"Are you okay?" Alex asked, his concern for me always at the forefront of everything we did.

"Yeah. I'm fine," I assured both of them quickly.

"Let me know when you're ready for more," Dex said softly, his grip on my hips tightening.

"I don't think I'm ever going to be ready for how much cock you have," I teased, getting a chuckle out of both of them. "But I'm good if you want to keep going."

I closed my eyes and held my breath as Dex pushed in deeper, the feeling a mixture of pain and pleasure.

"Fuck," I whimpered, letting my head fall as I got used to the overly full sensation.

"Does it feel good?" Alex questioned as he trailed his fingers softly up and down my arms.

I nodded and opened my eyes to find him watching me.

"It feels amazing."

I smiled at him and then looked over my shoulder to smile at Dex. He chewed the corner of his lower lip before pulling out slightly and thrusting back in, making my back arch as I tried to get more.

"Hold tight, baby. It's going to get a lot better," Dex said reassuringly, his smile mischievous and filled with desire.

I wasn't sure how it would work with both of their cocks inside of me, but then I remembered that they had done this before. It wasn't surprising when they both started moving in a rhythm that was perfectly balanced so neither of them slipped out. I tried to grind my hips and get the friction that I craved, but then Alex took care of that by rubbing my clit with his thumb and nearly sent me over the edge on impact.

My eyes fluttered closed as I let out a deep sigh and enjoyed the feeling of complete fullness while my husband and his best friend fucked me senseless.

Twenty-Five
Alex

"How are you feeling?" I asked Georgia as she laid in my arms, her head resting against my chest.

Dex and I had already taken care of cleaning her up and made sure she was comfortable before we all piled into the bed, pinning Georgia in between us.

"Tired," she replied sleepily as she struggled to fight a yawn.

I felt Dex's eyes on me and knew he was worried about how Georgia felt after what had happened. Even though we had all talked about it and checked in with each other several times, that didn't mean that something couldn't change after it happened.

"I really liked having both of your cocks inside of me at the same time," Georgia continued softly, her eyes closed as her body relaxed into the mattress. "I'm happy that we did that, and I can't wait to have both of you at the same time again."

Dex let out a sigh of relief that was loud enough to make Georgia smile.

"Lie down," she said to him, patting the spot right beside her while her eyes stayed closed. "You're making me nervous with you sitting there watching me."

"I just care about you," Dex replied gently as he lowered himself and laid down beside her.

"I know. And I appreciate that. But I'm too tired to worry about anything right now. I feel good. I had fun. Now I want to sleep in my new favorite place."

"Oh yeah? Where's that?" I asked, rubbing my hand soothingly across her hip.

"Sandwiched in between my two favorite men."

She smiled, but her eyes didn't open again as she quickly drifted to sleep.

I chuckled and got comfortable as Dex and I followed suit behind her.

****

The next day, Dex and I worked on things around the cabin, tackling the guest room that had been used as a catch-all room for everything that didn't have a place. I tried not to let my frustration get to me that my grandmother had allowed it to get this out of hand before she asked for help, then I reminded myself that she hadn't been herself for a while now and likely didn't realize what was happening.

"Where do you want me to put all of this?" Dex asked as he held up a box full of random kitchen gadgets that must have been in the cabinets before they were replaced.

"Would you mind taking them to Georgia and seeing if she can help find a place for them? She loves organization, and I'm sure she's getting bored."

"I don't know. Last time I saw her, she was devouring another book. We might have lost her to steamy romance books for good," Dex teased, grinning as he took the box out to the living room where she was sitting on the couch.

I kept working, shaking my head when I lifted a tarp from a stack of boxes and found a pile of supplies beneath it. Sure enough, everything that we needed to work on the guest bathroom had already been purchased and was sitting right there.

"She was so excited to organize the drawers that she squealed and abandoned her book," Dex said with a laugh as he came into the room.

"I'm glad she has found happiness with kitchen utensils. I, however, have found pure joy with this." I stepped back and pulled the rest of the tarp off, showing him the supplies.

"You've got to be kidding me. It was here the whole time?"

"It appears so."

"Well, at least we can get that project done without having to wait to get back down the mountain."

"Yeah. It seems someone had grabbed everything and started the work, they just never got it finished."

"Did your grandmother say why?"

I shook my head and shoved a hand through my hair.

"Nope. She didn't even remember hiring anyone. My mom found a charge on her bank statement and had to ask her about it."

"Well, hopefully we have everything we need. If not, we should be able to get the little stuff at the general store."

"I guess we won't know until we get started."

"Let's go," Dex said, nodding his head as he headed out of the room and down the short hallway to the guest bathroom.

I followed behind him, ready to get some of the projects completed so we could focus on more enjoyable stuff, like fucking Georgia.

Twenty-Six

Georgia

It felt like the days flew by as the guys worked on the guest bathroom. I was happy that they found all of the supplies they needed, but I couldn't lie and say that I wasn't bored out of my mind while they were working. If we were at home, I would have plenty of stuff to keep me busy. Or maybe it had nothing to do with being stuck in a cabin and everything to do with two sexy men who insisted on working without their t-shirts because it was too hot. So what if I *accidentally* kept bumping the heater up? A girl had needs.

By the fifth day of the guest bathroom renovation, I felt like I was going to go out of my mind. We'd been stuck in the cabin for what felt like weeks, and while it was fun to have sex and play around with each other, I missed being able to go outside and get fresh air.

I was curled up on the couch, staring at the TV when Alex came into the living room and tossed my boots on the floor beside me.

"Put your shoes on," he said as he grabbed his coat from the rack and pulled it on.

"Why?" I asked, tossing the blanket to the side as I put them on.

"We need a few things from the general store to finish the bathroom. I thought maybe you'd like to get out for a little bit today. Maybe have lunch in town?"

"Are you kidding me?" I asked, my eyes wide with disbelief.

"Nope. Not even a little. The weather is supposed to be nice today, so we should have a full day before the snow returns."

"And we get to go to a real store? Not like one of those boring stores where all they have is nuts and bolts and stuff?" I asked, taking my jacket as he handed it to me.

"No," he replied with a laugh. "It's a general store. While they have nuts and bolts and stuff, they also have other things. Like groceries and houseware stuff."

"Do they have gift type things?" I pressed as I stood up and allowed him to help me put my jacket on. I pulled my hair out and tossed it behind my shoulder as his eyes glinted with mischief.

"Are you asking me to buy you a present?"

"Nope. I thought maybe I could start my Christmas shopping. I don't know if we'll still be stuck up here by the time Christmas comes, but I hate the thought of spending it up here and no one having anything to open Christmas morning."

"We can do some shopping," he promised as he leaned forward and kissed the tip of my nose.

I squealed and clapped my hands excitedly as Dex walked in.

"You told her she can do some shopping?" he asked Alex with an ear-to-ear grin.

"I did," Alex confirmed.

"I'm glad to see how happy she is about it."

"Why wouldn't I be happy?" I grabbed Dex's arm and held onto it as we walked to the front door. "I get to leave the cabin and go to a store and see real people. I get to breathe in the fresh air and touch everything I want to on the shelves."

"Remind me later to dress up as an elf," Dex teased as he grabbed his coat and wiggled his eyebrows.

I frowned, my eyebrows pinched together in confusion.

"Since you want to touch everything on the shelves, I can pretend to be an elf on the shelf."

I rolled my eyes and laughed as I shook my head.

"You know you don't have to go to those lengths to get me to touch you."

"True. But role playing might be fun."

"And a tiny elf is what turns you on?"

He scrunched his face as he considered it.

"No. Not really. It's pretty much just the thought of you touching me. Maybe while wearing some sexy lingerie. We should look for some while we're there," Dex mused.

"We don't need to. That's all Georgia packed to sleep in when we came up here. She has a whole stash in the drawer," Alex offered.

My face flushed with heat as I stared at him. I reached over and smacked him in the chest, not sure why I was so mad at him.

"What?" he asked with a laugh, raising his hands to keep me from smacking him again.

"Why did you say that?" I hissed. "That's private."

"I hate to break it to you, baby, but there's nothing private between us anymore," Dex whispered in my ear, loud enough for Alex to hear. His hand skimmed my waist, making sure I felt his touch enough to miss it once it was gone. "I can't wait to see you wear it when we get home."

"I never said that I was going to wear it," I rushed out, suddenly feeling super embarrassed.

"Why not?" Dex asked, shoving his hands in his pockets as he rocked back on his heels. He looked far too sexy in his distressed jeans and snug T-shirt that highlighted all of my favorite parts of him. "I've seen and touched and tasted almost every inch of your body, Georgia. Why can't I see you in some lingerie?"

He licked his lips and my body nearly burst into flames.

"I don't know," I blurted out, shaking my head to clear the chaotic mess my brain was creating.

"How about this?" He stepped closer and rested his hands on my waist as his eyes locked onto mine. "We'll look at a few things together at the store and see if there's something that you like. Maybe you can pick something just for me, and in return, I'll do something for you."

"Like what?" I murmured.

His eyes darkened as he leaned in and whispered in my ear so only I could hear.

"I'll let you tie me up and do anything you want to me."

I swallowed hard as he stepped back, smirking when he saw the desire washing over me. He wasn't playing fair, and he knew it.

Twenty-Seven

Dex

Georgia was happier than a kid given unlimited access to all of the candy in the world. I grinned as I watched her zip past us with her shopping cart, her face lit up with happiness as the contents in the cart almost spilled over.

"Should we try to stop her?" I asked Alex, my voice laced with a playful tone.

I had no intention of trying to stop her or put a damper on her happiness.

"I'd like to see you try," he replied with raised eyebrows as he tossed a handful of supplies we needed for the guest bathroom into the cart.

Ours was much smaller compared to Georgia's, with only the essential things we needed. I knew that she was doing her Christmas shopping, which made her beyond happy. I wanted to take some time to look around for things to get her for Christmas, but I wasn't sure if that was going to be weird now.

I'd always gotten something for Georgia for Christmas ever since she and Alex started dating. The difference was that it was usually a scented candle or a new throw blanket for the couch. Something you could give your grandmother without worrying about it. Now that I'd fucked her and could still taste her on my tongue, I had no idea what the gift-giving should look like this year. It felt like a dick move to get her something as impersonal as a candle, but I didn't want to overstep and give her something that her husband would give her.

"You're overthinking it," Alex said, startling me.

"Overthinking what?"

"Whatever has your face all scrunched up like that."

He added a few light plate covers to the cart and then pushed it down the aisle, forcing me to follow him.

"I don't know what to get Georgia for Christmas this year," I admitted, shoving my hands in my pockets to keep from fidgeting.

"Georgia always loves the gifts you give her."

"I know. But it's… different now."

He stopped and pulled over to the side of the aisle as he studied my face.

"Why? Because you fucked her?"

Panicked, I quickly looked around to make sure no one had heard him.

"Look, I know things have changed between the three of us, but the one thing that has stayed the same is the love that you and Georgia have always had for each other. She will love whatever you decide to get her."

I let my shoulders fall as I pushed out a frustrated breath because even though he was right, that didn't make it any easier to know what to get her.

"I need to go grab a few groceries," he said as I stood there, still contemplating ideas. "I spotted a book section by the greeting cards on the way in."

He winked and pushed the cart as if he didn't just give me the best fucking idea in the world.

I practically jogged over to the area he was talking about, excitement flooding through me when I realized this was the perfect gift. Georgia loved to read, and we had started to share a love for it together with me reading some of her books. She had finally finished Third Time's The Charm and let me have it, which I was thankful for. I started it at the beginning and found that I was quite the bookworm when I couldn't put it down.

I stopped at the books and my eyes quickly scanned the options, thoroughly impressed with how many books they had for being up in the middle of nowhere. I shoved a hand through my hair and stared, trying to remember what books Georgia said she had already read.

"Shopping for your girlfriend?" a woman my age asked as she set a book back onto the shelf.

"Is it that obvious?" I asked with a laugh as she turned to face me. I didn't bother correcting either of us about whether Georgia was my girlfriend. It seemed like the easier thing to go with than to obsess over what she was to me right now.

"Only a tiny bit." She laughed and switched the cart she was holding to her other arm. "Do you need help?"

"Do you read steamy romance?" The last thing I wanted was to buy a bunch of books without any spice in them and then disappoint Georgia. Okay, okay. Disappoint *myself.*

"I do. Pretty much exclusively. Do you know what she tends to like?"

I shoved my hand through my hair again, already feeling lost and overwhelmed. I knew what Georgia liked in bed, but not so much regarding what kind of books she liked to read.

"I've only read one of them so far," I admitted.

"You read her book?" Her voice lifted as if she were genuinely impressed by this.

"I did. It was spicy. There was a cucumber, and they had a safe word. It was okra." I pressed my lips together to keep from talking because I was doing nothing but rambling and embarrassing myself.

She lifted her free hand and covered her mouth as she giggled.

"Remind me to get the name of that book before I leave," she teased, pointing her finger at me before she turned back to the shelf. Her eyes moved as quickly as her fingers as they brushed against the spines of the books before pulling one out. "Does she like sex club stuff?"

I shrugged my shoulders.

"I don't know. But I can't imagine that she wouldn't," I answered.

"This one is really good. There's a scene with shibari, which could be really fun if you guys are acting out anything from the books."

I smiled and took the book from her, looking at the cover that had one woman and three shirtless men on it.

"Does she get with…" I let my thought trail off as I felt my cheeks flame with embarrassment.

"She does. Room Fifteen is part of the Club Sin Chicago series, but honestly, I'll read anything that Elyse Kelly writes."

"Thank you. I will gladly take your recommendation," I said with a warm smile, clutching the book to my chest.

She returned the smile and then went back to looking at the books before selecting a few and leaving. I spent longer than I should have in the book section, but by the time Alex found me, I had ten different books for Georgia that I thought she would love.

He grinned and nodded his head in approval as I added them to the top of the cart and then covered them with my jacket to keep Georgia from seeing them.

We finished our shopping and checked out separately, so we didn't see what Georgia was buying. This also meant she couldn't see the books and other gifts I had bought for her. She was so damn cute with how excited she was that I didn't bother commenting on how she bought eight rolls of wrapping paper. I knew she would send us off to work on something as soon as we got home, or she would lock herself in the bedroom while she wrapped the gifts she purchased.

Little did she know, I was already planning to be busy the rest of the afternoon. Not only were we finishing the guest bathroom, but I was also going to make a special dinner that I knew she would love.

Twenty-Eight
Alex

My stomach rumbled as I waited impatiently for Dex to finish making dinner. I knew how much Georgia loved his prime rib and garlic mashed potatoes, so it didn't surprise me any when I saw him grabbing the stuff at the store to make it tonight.

Georgia had spent a solid hour in the bedroom after we got home and threatened us both with no blow jobs for a week if we walked in on her. I knew how much she loved giving gifts and would never spoil the surprise for her. Since there was nothing else to do while Dex cooked and Georgia finished her stuff, I made myself useful and cleaned up some of the guest room. Just as I was finishing up, Georgia came out of the master bedroom and stopped me dead in my tracks in the hallway.

"Holy fucking hell, baby," I groaned, leaning against the wall for support as I looked her up and down.

"Do you think he'll like it?" she asked as she nervously ran her hands down the front of the green velvet-looking bodysuit that hugged her curves perfectly. A sheer red skirt wrapped snugly around her waist, showing off the high-cut material that barely covered her pussy.

"He's going to love it. Turn around, let me see the back," I said, my voice hoarse as I twirled my finger in a circular motion.

She did as I asked, moving slowly as I took in every inch of her beautiful body. The bodysuit not only had a deep, plunging neckline in the front, but it appeared to be a thong, which would drive Dex wild.

"You look so fucking sexy, Georgia. I love this. Remind me to buy you more lingerie like this."

"It was hard to find much at the store, but I brought this one from home and thought it kinda looked like an elf…"

"You had this at home?" I asked, pushing off the wall to touch her as my eyebrows lifted in surprise.

"I was going to surprise you with it on the trip," she whispered as she leaned into my touch when my hands wrapped around her waist. "It has crotchless panties."

I let my head fall back as my dick hardened immediately. My hand slid down her side and across her hip before landing on her pussy. She stepped slightly to the side, allowing my fingers to brush against her slit.

I blew out a frustrated breath and pulled my hand back, knowing that once I touched her, I wouldn't be able to stop.

"He's going to fucking love this," I promised her, giving her a little bit of space as Dex came around the corner and stopped suddenly when he saw her.

"Fuck. Me." His eyes quickly roamed over her body, taking in every tiny detail. I laughed when I saw the way his face changed the second he realized that she was wearing crotchless panties. "I came to tell you guys that dinner is ready."

"Perfect. I'm famished," Georgia said, her voice beyond flirty as she shifted and attempted to walk past us to the kitchen.

"I don't fucking think so," Dex growled as he grabbed her by the waist and stopped her.

"What's wrong?" Georgia asked, playing innocent like she didn't know the effect she was having on both of us.

"The only thing I'm planning to eat right now is this pussy, Georgia. I'm not a patient man, so don't test me."

My shoulders shook as I laughed, loving the way Georgia's face lit up as Dex's hands were on her.

"But you worked so hard on dinner. It smells so good. You can't make me wait to eat, Dex," she said as she stuck her lower lip out and pouted.

"You can't make me wait to eat either, Georgia," he said gruffly as he dropped to his knees in front of her. "Fuck, this is so hot."

His fingers trailed over the fabric of the sheer skirt before he undid it and dropped it to the floor. Then he guided her against the wall and helped her spread her legs before he leaned in and swiped his tongue along her slit.

She hissed out a breath that turned into a moan as she closed her eyes and dug her nails into his hair. He reached up and lifted her until her pussy was perfectly lined up against his mouth, her legs hanging over his shoulders.

My dick got painfully hard as I watched him devour her without mercy, sucking and licking as she moaned and writhed against his face.

I leaned in, gripped her throat, and kissed her, my tongue sliding over her lips until she parted them and let me in. My hand skimmed her breast, loving how full they felt in the flimsy fabric that struggled to contain them.

"Baby, you look so fucking hot in this outfit, but seeing you pinned to the wall while Dex eats your pussy is threatening to send me over the edge," I growled as I pulled away from her lips and lowered my mouth to her breast, pulling her pebbled nipple into my mouth and sucking.

"Fuck!" she panted, arching her back as Dex pressed harder, flicking her clit with his tongue until she spasmed around it while I continued sucking her nipple with just enough pressure to border on painful. She moaned loudly, the sound of it making me desperate to come inside of her as I pulled away and stared at her, completely in awe of how beautiful she looked coming undone from the hands—and mouth—of my best friend.

Her body went limp as soon as she was done. Dex pulled his face back and gently helped her get back on her feet before he stood up and wiped the corners of his mouth.

"Alright. Like I said, dinner is ready."

"You just ate," Georgia objected, a faint blush on her cheeks as I reached for her hand and held it.

"That was just an appetizer." He winked and chewed his lower lip.

"Well, I guess I should go change for dinner." Georgia looked down at what she was wearing, then caught our eyes.

"I don't think so. I think you should stay in that and maybe I'll fuck you at the dinner table again," I offered, pulling her into my side.

"I think I like the sound of that." She giggled and leaned up to kiss me on the cheek before we followed Dex into the kitchen for a meal that was sure to please.

Twenty-Nine

Georgia

If you would have told me that someday I would be sitting at the dinner table in my husband's grandmother's cabin, wearing sexy lingerie while eating prime rib with him and his best friend—I would have said you were out of your mind. How we got to this point—I had no idea. Okay, so maybe I had a teeny tiny idea.

It all started when Dex asked me to wear lingerie for him. There was something in his eyes that made me want to do it for him, to give him that pleasure. I had struggled to find something at the store, but then remembered there were a few new things I had purchased and brought with us on the trip. Though that was before I knew anything would happen with Dex.

Even with Dex constantly complimenting and worshipping my body, that didn't stop the overwhelming self-conscious feelings I had when I put the outfit on. I had only meant to try it on, not to stay wearing it. But then once I had it on and Alex saw it, I knew there was no turning back. If I hadn't let Dex see it right then and there, I wouldn't have put it on again, because the fear of putting myself on display like that was too much.

We all took our time eating—which was surprising given the amount of tension in the room. Both of them gripped their forks and knives harder than needed, and I imagined they were trying to restrain themselves as much as I was. While I was literally battling hunger pains and needed the nourishment, I needed their cocks even more.

They worked on cleaning up while I was told to sit and rest until they were done, something I would never quite understand. It wasn't like putting dishes in the dishwasher was strenuous or anything, yet they treated me like I was some delicate flower who needed to be guarded and protected.

I picked up the book I had been reading and got comfy, knowing that they would interrupt as soon as I got to the good part. But then again, the entire book was spicy, so it wasn't like I had to wait long.

I had gotten so deep into the book that I had totally forgotten that I was still wearing the lingerie and didn't notice Dex as he plopped down beside me and started trailing his fingers up my thigh.

"Read me what you're reading." He nodded to where I was clutching it against my chest as my cheeks flamed with embarrassment.

No. Fucking. Way.

There was absolutely no way I could read this one to him. To either of them. It was like porn wrapped up in the beautiful disguise of literature. I knew they would never stop giving me shit about this book and how much it turned me on.

"I'm waiting," he added, his voice as stern as the look he pinned me with.

"Dex…" I objected with an awkward laugh. "I'm sure there's something else you'd rather do than listen to me read this book to you." I rolled my eyes for dramatic effect, panicking when I noticed the look he gave me.

"Actually, there's nothing I would love more than to hear you read it to me." He leaned back against the couch and stretched his arms above his head before linking them behind his head as he got fully relaxed.

I tipped my head back slightly and exhaled heavily. There was no way I could read *this* out loud to *him* and still be able to hide how much it turned me on—especially since I was still wearing the sexy elf lingerie that was missing the panty portion.

"I actually peeked at the book this morning while you were in the shower," Alex said, joining us as he sat in the chair across from us. "It's pretty hot. What chapter are you on?"

I met his stare for a moment before I lowered my eyes and thumbed back a handful of pages until I found it.

"Chapter seven."

"I don't think I read anything that far in. Why don't you read it for all of us?"

I narrowed my eyes and glared at my husband. He was supposed to save me and come to my rescue. Not feed me to the shark, AKA, his best friend.

"I really don't think you guys want to hear this one," I objected, hating how squeaky my voice sounded. "We can do something else instead. I was just reading for a few minutes while you guys finished cleaning, since you wouldn't let me help."

"Oh no," Dex said, waving his hand to stop me. "I can tell by the blush that hasn't left your skin that this is a *good* book. I can't wait to hear it."

I swallowed hard and blew out a heavy sigh, knowing I wasn't going to get out of this. I opened the book to the page I was on and felt my temperature climb even higher as I stared at the words on the page.

"Fine. Since neither of you is going to give it a break, I will read to you."

They both grinned, making me hate how adorable they are. It made it so much harder to be angry with them when they did that.

I cleared my throat and kept my eyes on the book to avoid their curious stares.

"Lay on my chest," I told her, making sure she was still okay. "It will help open you up for him." "Okay." She leaned forward, pressing her chest to mine as Josh lined himself up at her entrance. My cock twitched inside her as we both held still as he started to slowly push inside her. I guided her face to mine and pressed a kiss to her lips." There. Happy?" I closed the book and looked between them, hoping this would satisfy their need to have me read to them.

"Nope. Keep going. It sounds like we were just getting to the good part," Alex said, leaning back and resting his arms over his chest.

"You're terrible." I shook my head and found Dex's lazy smile as he waited impatiently for me to continue. *"You're doing so good, baby. Take a deep breath and try to relax, he's almost all the way in." Josh waited a second for her to relax around us before he slid in the rest of the way, our cocks rubbing against each other as her pussy gripped us greedily. "Fuck, baby," Josh grunted, holding onto her hips as he slowly began thrusting."* There. That's all I'm reading." I closed the book and set it on the coffee table, hoping neither of them had seen the evidence of my arousal when I moved.

"My, my, my. That's quite the book you're reading, Georgia," Dex said playfully, his hand back to teasing my skin as he trailed it up and down my thigh.

I wanted to look away, to pretend like the words on the page hadn't affected me. But I couldn't. Once Dex's eyes caught mine, I was trapped, and there was no going back. He held my gaze as his hand inched higher, his finger teasing my pussy as it slid through the wetness that had pooled between my legs.

"Do you want to try it?" Alex asked, clearing his throat after his voice came out hoarse.

I rubbed my lips together, considering my answer. We'd already done it with one of them in each of my holes, and I loved it—but would it be painful to try it with both of them in the *same* hole?

"I don't know," I admitted, feeling my skin get clammy as a sheen of sweat covered it. "Have you guys done that before?"

I knew it was always risky talking about sexual experiences that happened outside of your relationship with the person you were with, but I felt like we were all past that point now. We'd crossed so many lines already, and I didn't find myself feeling even a bit of jealousy knowing that they'd both shared women before Alex and I got together.

"Yes," Alex answered while Dex nodded his head.

"And you both enjoyed it?"

This time they both nodded their head.

"Is it going to hurt?" I tried to keep my face from scrunching up, but the thought of taking both of their cocks in a hole that wasn't designed for such large *cargo* had me a bit worried.

"We'll always do everything we can to keep anything from hurting you, Georgia," Dex quickly assured me, his hand resting on my thigh.

I knew then that his words went deeper than just any possible physical pain associated with what we were talking about. He meant that on a whole other level, which made my heart love him more than I should have.

Thirty

Dex

"I told you I wasn't lying," I said to Georgia as she studied the rope in my hands.

"I don't even know how to do this," she whispered, staring at it.

"You can do it however you want to. You're not going to hurt me."

She cocked her head to the side and pinned me with a look that called me on my bullshit.

"Okay—you *can* hurt me with it. But I trust that you won't. Besides, Alex can help you."

"You've tied someone up before?" she asked, turning to face her husband as his face flushed with color.

"Maybe?" He scrunched his face, which only earned a playful smack on his arm from her.

"Why haven't you ever told me?"

"I don't know, baby." He shrugged and let his shoulders fall. "When I'm with you, I'm not thinking about stuff I used to do with other women. I'm more concerned with being in the moment with *you*. With discovering what things I need to do to make you scream my name as you drip down your thighs while you wait for me to make you come harder than you ever have before."

"Stop it," she hissed, pointing a finger at him.

"Stop what?" he asked with a laugh.

"Stop lowering your voice and slowly creeping toward me. I can't get all turned on right now. I'm trying to figure something important out and I don't need you clogging my brain with your—your—sexiness." She threw her hands in the air in frustration.

"Have I ever told you how cute you are when you're mad?" I asked, feeling the dimple in my cheek deepen with my grin.

"Do you want me to hurt you?" she threatened, but I could see the playfulness she was trying to keep from us.

I shrugged my shoulder and gave her a nonchalant look.

"I mean… maybe. I like a little pain sometimes."

"You're impossible," she breathed out, frustrated.

"Don't knock it until you try it," I whispered, lifting her chin with my finger as I slowly lowered my lips over hers.

She whimpered softly, her body immediately giving in to my touch.

While she was distracted, I slid my hand up her side and gently caressed her breast before pulling the fabric of the lingerie down so her nipple was exposed. I tilted my head, deepening the kiss as her hands locked behind my neck. Then I brushed my fingers over her nipple, loving how it hardened right away. Her tongue teased my mouth, begging for more as I pinched my fingers around her nipple, increasing the pressure until she gasped and pulled away.

A mix of emotions crossed her face as she stared at me in disbelief.

I waited a few seconds for her to process what had just happened, but more so, for her to figure out how she felt about it. The rope felt heavy in my other hand as I waited her out, watching as her skin flushed with color.

"That wasn't very nice," she said, her voice slightly shaky.

"I beg to differ," I responded, chewing my lower lip. "I bet if I were to touch you right now, you'd be drenched from how turned on that made you."

"I've been turned on for hours. It's nothing new."

I chuckled and tried to hide it when I felt her glare at me. I knew it had been a while since I'd eaten her out against the wall, but *hours* was a bit of a stretch, especially since we all could have earned a medal for how fast we devoured dinner. No one was trying to waste any time getting to the good stuff tonight.

"I see that bratty attitude is making a comeback. Do I need to fix it for you again?" I offered, knowing that she just needed to be pushed right now.

"How about I fix yours instead?" she asked, one hand on her hip while she held the other in front of her and waited for me to hand her the rope.

"By all means, baby." I grinned and raised an eyebrow, challenging her as she took it from me. "Where do you want me?"

"The same spot you made me sit," she instructed, pointing to the bed.

I knew that the rope she was going to use had a guaranteed chance of hurting me and giving me rope burn, but I wasn't going to tell her that and ruin this for her. I had promised her that if she wore lingerie for me, I would let her tie me up. I was a man of my word, even if I wished that I had brought my other rope up here. Though that would have been weird, given that none of us could have predicted that any of this would happen.

"You know what would be even hotter than tying Dex up with that rope?" Alex said in Georgia's ear as he stood behind her and rubbed his hands soothingly down her arms.

"What?"

"If you used your panties instead."

"My panties?" Georgia turned around and looked at him, confusion written all over her face.

"Mmm hmm. They're more gentle than the rope, and it'll drive him wild knowing that they've touched your pussy. Maybe grab a few pairs of the silk ones. Those would be nice."

I grinned, loving how he so subtly had my back with this one. But then again, it wasn't the first time we'd used rope when we shared a woman before, so he knew the risks with using what we had.

Georgia set the rope down and went to the dresser, pulling a few pairs of panties out before looking at them and putting them back. I wasn't sure what she was up to until I saw her pull out something that looked like black leather.

She held it against her body and looked at me, a wicked smile crossing her face.

"You know, the whole elf thing was fun, but I think maybe we should change things up a bit," she teased. "Do you want to help me change?" She turned to Alex, holding up the piece of lingerie while I sat on the bed and waited.

It was pure torture to see him touching her body as he helped her out of one outfit and into the other—which I'm sure was why she did it. She wanted to pay me back for pinching her nipple and I couldn't wait. My dick hardened at the thought of what she might do to me once I was tied up and at her mercy.

Georgia finished getting dressed and turned to face me while Alex pulled the ribbons in the back, pulling the corset tighter and forcing her breasts on display. I swallowed hard, loving how she looked like a fucking dominatrix and I wanted nothing more than for her to use me for her pleasure.

"Are you ready?" she asked, picking up two pairs of panties from the drawer and holding them in her hand.

"I can't fucking wait," I responded, licking my lips.

"Clothes off," she demanded with a smirk that looked adorable on her.

I lowered my head and tried to fight my grin as I did what she asked. Once my clothes were tossed into a pile on the floor, I scooted back to where she wanted me and waited.

"I think he should be tall enough to secure him to the hooks without needing the rope," Alex said, nodding to the wall as Georgia climbed on the bed and headed toward me. Her pussy would soon be lined up with my face, and there was no way the thin, see-through pair of black panties would keep me away.

She stood up, accepting my hand as I tried to steady her. Once she was good, I slowly let my hands slide down her thighs, touching her as much as I could before she took that away from me.

"Get on your knees and give me your hand," she said, her voice soft even though I could tell she was trying to sound in control.

I lifted my arm and watched as she wrapped the panties around my wrist and tied them tightly.

"Do you think the knot will come undone?" Georgia asked Alex as she looked over her shoulder at him.

"Not if you do it like this," he replied, coming to stand next to her on the bed as he showed her how to pull them through in a way that they couldn't come undone. He helped her get the other hand restrained, then pulled on them before securing them to the hook. He shook his head as he climbed down and moved out of Georgia's way.

"I think I like you like this," she said, running a finger along the stubble on my jaw.

"I think I like it too," I replied, wiggling my eyebrows as I glanced down at my erection.

Her eyes lit up, but she looked away before saying anything.

"Maybe just one more thing," she said, more to herself than to us.

She climbed off the bed and walked back to the dresser, getting another pair of panties. Then she climbed up beside me and pressed her thumb down on my chin, forcing my mouth open as she shoved them inside.

"There. That's better."

She smiled an innocent smile, but I knew that deep down she was a wicked, wicked woman.

Thirty-One
Georgia

I was practically dripping as I felt Dex's cock against my stomach as I shoved my panties into his mouth. Seeing him on his knees, tied up, did something to me. I slowly slid down onto my hands and knees and looked up at him from under my lashes as I took my time licking the drop of precum off the tip of his cock.

He closed his eyes and hissed, his body tensing against my touch. I reached down and pushed my panties to the side, knowing that Alex was loving this view. Keeping my balance, I used one hand to hold Dex's dick as I sucked it while lowering the other one between my legs and playing with my pussy.

I heard Alex behind me grunting and knew that he was struggling not to touch me until I told him he could. I loved that both of them were willing to give me anything I wanted or desired, even if it meant putting their pleasure on hold.

I pulled Dex out of my mouth for a second as I looked over my shoulder at Alex.

"Why don't you come fuck me while I suck your best friend's cock?" I batted my eyes and chewed my lower lip as I watched him rush to undress.

I turned my attention back to Dex, slowly stroking the base of his cock while my tongue played with the tip. Then I felt the mattress dip as Alex climbed up behind me, his hands rubbing down my back before gripping my hips.

"Fuck, baby. You're so wet and ready for me," he said as he lined himself up at my entrance and thrust inside.

I cried out in pure pleasure as he filled me, immediately pulling out and thrusting in again. He knew how much I loved when he did this, so I focused on stroking Dex's cock while Alex fucked me hard and rough—just how I wanted it.

My body was tense and begging for a release, but I wasn't ready to stop torturing Dex just yet. Alex slowed his thrusts, keeping them hard but steady as I took Dex's cock back into my mouth, gagging as he hit the back of my throat.

He groaned, his muscles tense, showing me how much he wanted to touch me, but couldn't. I hollowed out my cheeks and sucked harder, bringing him right to the edge before pulling away.

"Fuck. Georgia," Alex panted. "I have to stop or I'm going to come."

"I think everyone deserves to come," I said sweetly. "But I want it to happen when both of you are inside of me."

"Fuck," Alex grunted, gripping my hips tighter as he forced himself to pull out.

I stroked Dex's cock a few more times before letting go and taking the panties out of his mouth. I wanted to play more with him being tied up, but I also needed to come, and I wanted to do so while riding both of their cocks.

"That was fucking hot, Georgia," Dex said with a huge grin on his face. "Remind me to have you tie me up more often."

"Unhook him, please," I whispered to Alex while I quickly removed my panties, a flush of heat rushing over my skin from the way Dex continued to look at me.

Alex nodded and made quick work of releasing Dex.

"Okay, how do you want to do this?" Alex asked, both of them looking to me for guidance.

"I don't know." I shrugged. It wasn't like I knew all of the ways in which to take two cocks in one hole at the same time.

"Do you want to lie down and hold her on top of you with her facing me?"

"That works for me," Dex said, looking to Alex.

Dex nodded and adjusted on the bed, lying down and watching me. He was close enough to the edge that his legs hung over the side.

"Whenever you're ready," he said softly.

I nodded and slowly moved over to where he was lying, turning myself so I was facing Alex. Then I lowered myself onto his cock, closing my eyes as I felt the immediate fullness.

His fingers dug into my skin as he held onto me, waiting until I was fully seated. Then he guided my feet to rest on his thighs, forcing my knees up to my chest as my legs spread wider.

"Okay," I said breathlessly, letting myself relax the best I could. I leaned back as much as I could and braced my hand next to Dex's head on the bed as I watched Alex. "Now your turn."

Alex grinned and stroked his cock that was already glistening with my arousal.

"You have to open up for him, baby," Dex said softly. "Remember how she did in the book? Let's spread those legs and let him in."

I tried to force my muscles to stop tensing as Dex's hands gently caressed my thighs as he pulled them open.

"Fuck. This is so hot, baby. Do you want to see it?" Alex asked, stopping right at my entrance.

"See what?"

"Dex's cock inside of you."

I opened my mouth to speak, but words wouldn't come out, so I nodded. Alex reached over and grabbed his cell phone from the nightstand, taking his time with taking a picture. Early on in our marriage, we had played around with naughty photos and the occasional recording ourselves, but this was different. This was my husband taking a picture of his best friend's cock inside my pussy. The thought thrilled me and sent tingles up my spine.

"Look how fucking hot that is," Alex said, turning the phone to show us.

"You better get another one once you're inside," Dex replied. "That's something I would die to have as my screensaver."

Alex chuckled and held his phone up with one hand while using his other to guide himself to my opening.

"Don't tense up, baby," Dex said, guiding me. "Try to relax."

I blew out a heavy breath and closed my eyes as I felt the sting as Alex slid inside, pushing in right beside Dex. When I opened my eyes, I found him still with his phone in his hand, recording us. I knew that I was at a loss for words right now, but I was absolutely going to want to see that later.

"Does that feel good, baby?" Alex asked as he slowly rocked his hips and gently lifted my leg to rest on his shoulder.

I felt Dex's body shift beneath me as he lifted his hips, moving in the same rhythm as Alex. I couldn't speak. Couldn't breathe. Couldn't do anything but focus on how amazing it felt to have both of them inside of me at the same time.

"Fuck!" I cried when Alex shifted his position slightly, lining his cock up to rub against my clit as he moved.

"Shit," Dex hissed out. "You take us so good, baby."

"Right? Her pussy feels so fucking good wrapped around both of us," Alex agreed.

I closed my eyes and just let myself be in the moment as they both took control and fucked me the way I needed to be fucked. I was fuller than I had ever been before, and now that I had both of their cocks inside me at the same time, I couldn't imagine ever going back to just one.

I was already turned on and ready to go, so it didn't take much for me to go over the edge and straight to heaven. I tipped my head back and relaxed, not sure whose hands were on my breasts and whose dick was doing what. It felt so amazing that I clenched my pussy and squeezed both of them tighter as it spasmed around them, claiming every last ounce of cum as they both released inside of me.

Thirty-Two

Alex

Three weeks had passed in a hurry, and once we were back home in the city, I couldn't help but miss the time we had in the cabin. It wasn't like we didn't see Dex often, but it was different not sharing a room with him and having our own space again. The weather had cleared and we had a small window before the next storm rolled in, so we decided to head down while we still could.

As soon as we got home, Dex and I took an urgent job helping with repairs at a local nursing home. I had helped get all of the decorating stuff out for Georgia before I left, but I could tell her mood was off. I knew she had started to love the cabin as much as I did, which made me question whether it was the best idea to come back when we did. It was only a week until Christmas, and given how much she loved the holiday, I didn't want to mess it up by ruining whatever plans she had for celebrating it.

"You okay?" Dex asked as he passed me with a stack of two-by-fours slung over his shoulder.

We were currently working in the kitchen, where a waterline had broken and flooded the room months ago.

While they did their best to clean everything up, there had been a constant leak before the waterline broke, which led to mold infesting the cabinets and pantry area.

"Yeah. Why?" I answered, trying to ignore him as I stared at the wall and held my level against it, and then marked an X with the pencil.

"You seem distracted for one," he replied with a grunt as he set the wood down and then stared at me. "Two, I have no idea what you're trying to level since nothing is on the wall."

"I was making my marks." I raised my eyebrows and shook my pencil at him.

"So we're going to mount the countertop a solid five feet off the ground? Fantastic. I'm sure Ms. Beltran will appreciate that, given that she's all of four feet."

I turned my attention back to the wall and frowned, realizing he was right.

"Shit." I blew out a frustrated breath and tried to clear my head.

"Start talking," Dex said as he stood beside me and leveled me with a look. "What's going on?"

"I don't know. Nothing? Everything?" I shoved a hand through my hair and let my shoulders drop. "Things have felt off ever since we got home from the cabin. I can't tell if it's just me or if everyone is off. Georgia hasn't seemed like her happy-go-lucky self, but maybe I'm misreading things because *I* feel out of sorts."

"Is she okay?"

I loved his immediate concern for her, and that I never had to worry whether he truly loved her.

I nodded, not wanting to speak because I had no idea.

"I brought out the stuff to decorate the house a few days ago, and she hasn't touched it. I mean, the tree is up, but nothing else is decorated."

"Maybe she just hasn't gotten to it yet," he offered softly.

But the problem was that we both knew how much Georgia loved to decorate and how this wasn't like her.

"It's six days until Christmas," I replied a little too harshly. "She seemed a lot happier when we were stuck in the cabin, so maybe I screwed up by having us come back? Or, I don't know, maybe she was just happier because you were there. Or because we were constantly having fun and there wasn't anything to worry about at the cabin. I just can't put my finger on what is going on, but I miss my happy wife. I can't stop thinking about how the last time she was truly happy was when we were all living together in a tiny, cramped space."

Dex nodded but said nothing.

"What if I come over tonight and we have dinner together? We can even go out to eat. Maybe we all just need a reset," he suggested with hope in his eyes.

"I'll call Georgia once we're done with this and see what she wants to do."

"I wouldn't stress too much over it. Let's see what happens tonight and go from there," he said reassuringly as he clapped a hand on my shoulder and walked off.

We still had a ton of work to do, but I couldn't focus on any of it as I worried about what was going on with Georgia and prayed that she hadn't started to regret what we had done at the cabin.

Thirty-Three
Dex

Alex wasn't wrong when he said something seemed off with Georgia. She hadn't wanted to go out for dinner, so we compromised with me bringing pizza and staying in instead. She was bundled under a thick blanket on the couch when I got there, staring at the Christmas tree in the corner of the room, even though it wasn't turned on. I tried not to obsess over it or think too much about it, but something definitely felt off.

"Thanks for bringing pizza," Georgia said as she climbed off the couch and came over to hug me in the kitchen. "It smells delicious."

"You're welcome," I replied, kissing the top of her head. "Although I was surprised you didn't want to go out tonight. I thought for sure you'd want to go to that steakhouse you love."

"I always love going there," she responded with a laugh. "It just felt weird to go in the middle of the week."

She pulled out a chair from the island and sat down, her features changing as she noticed the look Alex and I were giving her.

"What?" She laughed nervously and lifted her hands in front of her. "It just seems weird to go sit for hours at a steakhouse on a Wednesday night unless it's someone's birthday or an anniversary."

"It's not Wednesday, baby. It's Friday," Alex said softly as he stroked a hand up and down her arm.

"Wait—what? What are you talking about?" she asked, looking between us. "I swear it's Wednesday. You guys have been back to work for three days—"

"We went back on Wednesday," I replied gently. "Today is Friday."

Georgia covered her mouth and looked at us with something that looked like fear in her eyes before she jumped off the chair and ran down the hallway to their bedroom.

"Should we follow her?" I asked uncertainly.

Alex shook his head and let out a heavy exhale.

A few minutes later, Georgia returned holding a small packet looking thing in her hand.

"It's Wednesday," she whispered, her trembling fingers covering her lips as she turned the package of birth control to face us.

My stomach sank when I realized what was happening. Alex gently grabbed her by the elbow and lowered her to the chair as he took the packet from her and looked at it. I stood beside him, needing to see it for myself.

The packet was almost empty with only a few pills left in the week four row.

"What does that mean?" I asked Alex, pointing to it with my finger.

He licked his lips and looked at Georgia as he spoke.

"It means that Georgia should have started her period this week."

Both of her hands covered her mouth as she closed her eyes and started crying.

"So she's late?"

"I thought I was just a day late," she said as she took in a shuddered breath. "I've been waiting all day for it to come. Are you sure it's not Wednesday?"

Alex set the birth control packet on the island and pulled out his phone, turning it to show her the date.

"How did this happen?" she cried, letting her hands go from her face and holding them in the air beside her.

"It seems you might have missed a pill or two this month," Alex answered, keeping his voice soft and gentle.

"And now… and now…" she sobbed uncontrollably. "And now I'm pregnant?"

"It kinda appears that way. But we won't know for sure until you take a test. I can run out and grab one for you," he offered.

"I'll go," I rushed out, feeling anxious and flighty, but more so wanting to give them some privacy to talk about this.

"No," Georgia said, wiping her face with the backs of her hands. "You brought pizza, and I'm not going to let us ruin it by letting it get cold. If I'm pregnant, I'll still be knocked up after dinner, so let's all sit down and eat."

I nodded, fighting the urge to run over and hold her in my arms to make her feel better.

"How many slices would you like?" Alex asked her, holding the paper plate while he waited to serve her.

"One for now," she replied with a softness that matched how tired she looked.

Alex arched an eyebrow, quietly questioning why she wasn't eating more. Georgia loved pizza and could devour a large one by herself.

"I've been a little nauseous today." She pressed her lips together and looked down as she folded her hands in her lap.

Alex and I glanced at each other for a brief moment before he passed her plate to her. I grabbed a slice from the box and took a bite, the food tasting bitter on my tongue as I worried about Georgia and whether she was carrying *my* child.

Thirty-Four

Georgia

The pizza did nothing but give me heartburn and make me regret eating it. I knew I didn't want more than one piece, but since I hadn't eaten all day, I thought it would be good to eat two slices. Big mistake.

The guys had insisted on running to the store right after dinner to get me a pregnancy test. Imagine my surprise when they came back twenty minutes later with seven boxes of pregnancy tests, an assortment of different brands.

I appreciated their support, especially when they offered to help in any way they could, but I knew I needed to do this on my own. I was freaking out—and rightfully so—because we hadn't talked about having a baby. Not just me and Alex—but none of us had talked about what would happen if I got pregnant once we started messing around with Dex.

My fingers trembled as I struggled to hold the pregnancy test steady as I dipped it into the cup of urine. I held it there for a few seconds, as instructed on the box, then slowly pulled it out. My heart jumped in my chest as a pink line immediately appeared. I tried to remind myself that it was just the control line and that it would be pink regardless.

But before I could look away, I saw the test line also turning pink.

Without thinking about it, I flipped it over and laid it on the paper towel covering the counter with the other tests lined up. I refused to look at any of them as I rushed out of the bathroom and sat on the edge of the bed. Alex calmly sat in the chair by the window while Dex paced beside him.

"How long do they take?" Dex asked, looking from me to Alex.

"The boxes said anywhere between three to five minutes," Alex answered.

"Or some right away," I mumbled as I rocked back and forth, chewing my nail.

Without saying anything, Alex got up and walked into the bathroom. I held my breath as I waited while Dex stood beside me.

"What does it say?" Dex asked a few seconds later.

Alex peeked his head around the corner and grinned at both of us as he held up several tests.

"Well, it says that Georgia is pregnant."

"They're all positive?" Dex questioned, stepping forward to take a look as Alex handed them to him.

"Every single one," Alex said as he came out and stood in front of me, offering me his hand as he smiled warmly.

I took it and stood up, hiding my face against his chest as he held me tight.

"It's going to be okay," he whispered in my ear as my body shook. "Babies are a wonderful thing, my love. We'll call the doctor next week and get you an appointment so we can start figuring everything out."

I nodded and let out a sigh of relief that at least now I knew why I hadn't been feeling well. I thought it was just because I was depressed being back in the city and missed the cabin. Little did I know I accidentally brought back a little stowaway.

Thirty-Five
Alex

My wife was pregnant. She was going to have a baby, and I couldn't help but worry about whether it was *my* child. It wasn't like we didn't know the risk of having sex without using condoms while we were up at the cabin, but it never crossed my mind that the birth control might not work. Or more importantly, that for the first time I could recall, Georgia would forget to take a few of them.

I knew she hadn't done so on purpose. The look of devastation on her face when she realized it was Friday and not Wednesday said it all. She had been hoping that she was only one day late with her period, not several. While Georgia and I had always talked about someday starting a family, we hadn't stopped to have a conversation on what would happen if it ended up being my best friend's baby instead.

I laid in bed beside her, watching her sleep. It was later than I usually got up on the weekend, but she had been so restless most of the night that I stayed up to make sure she was okay. I knew it was a lot to process with finding out she was pregnant, but I didn't want to assume that I knew how she was feeling or what was going through her mind.

She shifted from her side and laid on her back as she let out a heavy sigh.

"I can feel you watching me."

I grinned, letting a soft chuckle escape.

"I like watching you," I replied as I continued doing so.

"I know you do. Usually it's when I'm doing something more interesting than just lying here in bed all knocked up." She turned her head and looked at me with such a deep sadness in her eyes.

I immediately scooted over and pulled her against my chest, wrapping her in my arms. She turned to face me, looking up as tears filled her eyes.

"What are we going to do?" she whispered, her lower lip beginning to tremble.

"About what?"

I knew my answer wasn't helpful, but I didn't want to dive down one rabbit hole if Georgia was headed for another one.

"What are we going to do if this baby isn't… if this baby is…" She pressed her lips together as a tear slid down her cheek.

"I don't have an answer for you on that," I replied honestly. "I don't think it's fair to decide anything until we have a chance to sit down and talk with Dex."

"What if it's his and he doesn't want to have a baby?"

"Then we'll cross that bridge when we get there. Either way, you're having a baby, Georgia, and I will be there by your side every single step of the way. You don't have to do any of this alone."

"I don't think I'm going to feel better about any of it until we know whose baby it is," she admitted. "I mean, how are you going to feel if the child I have isn't yours? What if you resent me and Dex because of this?"

"One—I could never resent either of you. What the three of us did was consensual, and we all knew the risks. Two— even if this baby is Dex's, that doesn't mean that I will love it any less. Three—there's an equal chance that this baby could be mine. We won't know for sure until the baby is born and we do a paternity test. But right now, the only thing that I'm worried about is you and making sure you're okay."

"How can I be okay? I'm knocked up and I don't even know who the father is." She laughed, but it was dry and humorless.

I lifted my hand and gently brushed my thumb across her cheek.

"It's a lot to process. I get it. But please stop beating yourself up over not knowing who the father is. You've barely known you were pregnant for like a day. There are so many other things that we need to worry about, like scheduling you a doctor's appointment and starting you on a prenatal vitamin. Knowing who the father is can wait, baby. I know that it makes you uneasy, but at the end of the day, you're carrying the baby of a man who loves you— regardless of who that might be. You're safe, and both Dex and I are going to make sure you are well taken care of throughout the entire pregnancy, and pretty much for the rest of your life."

"I honestly don't know what I did to deserve you," she said softly, placing her hand over mine and gently squeezing it.

My phone buzzed on the nightstand, distracting us. Even though I hated to, I pulled my hand away and grabbed it, already knowing it would be Dex.

"Dex wants to know if he can come hang out today. Maybe help with the rest of the Christmas decorations if you're up for it?"

"Sure. But he doesn't have to help with the decorations. I don't know if I even want to bother with putting them up when we're just going to turn around and take them down in a week."

I nodded because I got her logic, even if it didn't sound like Georgia. My fingers flew quickly across the screen as I responded to his message.

Just as I was about to set my phone down, it vibrated again.

"He wants to know if he can bring donuts and coffee," I said with a chuckle. He knew the key to Georgia's heart was with a maple-glazed donut.

"Ooooh! Can he bring me a few of those really giant maple ones?" she asked as her eyes lit up.

"I'll let him know to bring some extra."

She squealed and did her happy dance as I texted him back, letting him know to bring a few dozen. If maple donuts brought her even a small portion of happiness, I would make sure she had them.

Thirty-Six

Georgia

"You did not!" I shrieked as I tipped my head back and laughed, ignoring how sticky my hands were from the maple glaze on the donut. "Dex!"

"What? She was like seventy and didn't need the maple-glazed donuts anyway." He threw his hands up, but the dimple in his cheek when he grinned had me squeezing my legs together to keep from getting turned on.

"I cannot believe you stole her donuts," I said as I shook my head playfully. "And here I thought you were a nice guy."

"Well, you would be wrong. I'm actually a donut-stealing villain who robs old women of their sugary treats and then uses them to bribe my best friend's wife to get sexual favors." He wiggled his eyebrows and my stomach did a flippy-floppy thing that made me feel nervous.

There was something different about Dex this morning, and I couldn't put my finger on what it was. It might have been the double shot of espresso he got in his coffee this morning, or maybe it was the barista who wrote her phone number on the sticker and put a heart around his name. Either way, he was fun and flirty and all sorts of bad news for me right now.

"I hate to tell you, but you don't have to bribe Georgia," Alex said as he sat down beside me and took a giant bite of his chocolate Bavarian cream-filled donut. A dot of white kissed the corner of his lip before he slid his tongue out and swiped it off.

I shook my head as I tried to get myself to focus. *Now* wasn't the time to be lusting over either of them. I was pregnant and needed to have some honest conversations with both of them about what we were going to do and what the next steps would be. I didn't have time to get all dick-erpated—or whatever it was that Thumper got in *Bambi*.

"True, but that doesn't mean I don't like to spoil her with sweet treats when I can. The sexual favors are just an added bonus," Dex replied with a wink that sent a jolt of electricity straight to my vagina.

"Okay," I said with a little too much force as I pushed away the rest of the donut sitting on the plate in front of me. It was my second—no wait, was it my third? Either way, it didn't matter. I pushed back whatever number donut it was and stared at both of them, hoping they would see how serious I was and that I meant business. "We need to talk."

Dex nodded his head as he wiped his fingers on a napkin before swiping it against his mouth and crumpling it into a ball. Alex, on the other hand, decided it was appropriate to stick his tongue in the hole he made in his donut and eat it out. He locked eyes with me and showed no mercy as he devoured the fucking pastry better than he'd ever devoured me.

"Are you serious right now?" I asked, blinking quickly as if that would erase the image that was now permanently burned inside my brain.

"I am. You know I love donuts. Especially the cream-filled kind. They're the best." He leaned in and took another bite, this time pushing down on the donut from the backside, making the cream rush out. "Oh, looks like this one is a squirter."

He grinned while Dex chuckled and the flames coming out of my head grew hotter.

"I don't even know why I try," I muttered, pushing away from the table when he reached out and wrapped his arms around my waist, trapping me.

"I'm sorry," he said softly. "I was just playing."

He lowered me down onto his lap, earning a glare from me when I sat on something hard.

"Sorry. The thought of eating you out got to me," he admitted with a blush that crept up his face. "I'll behave. What do you want to talk about?"

Dex leaned back in his chair and rubbed a hand down his stomach, immediately drawing my attention to his chiseled abs that I knew were hiding underneath his t-shirt.

"I can't do this," I exclaimed, throwing my hands in the air as I looked at both of them with bewilderment. "You two are impossible!"

"What did I do?" Dex asked, his eyes wide but the corners of his lips curling up into a smile.

"You," I accused as I pointed at him. "You're just sitting there, rubbing your chest and stomach as if I'm not going to stare at it and remember how fucking hot it is when you don't wear a shirt. And you," I said, turning to face Alex, "are sitting here with a fucking erection poking into my ass after making me watch you eat out a donut!"

"Okay, okay," Alex said, lifting his hands in defense as he laughed. "We'll be good. I promise."

I narrowed my eyes and looked at both of them, challenging them. When they sat still with their hands folded in their laps, I took my seat—away from Alex's lap—I couldn't be trusted to act or think right with that thing on the loose.

"Alright," I said, sighing heavily as I rested my hands on the table. "As we already know, I am pregnant. There really isn't a big surprise as to how this happened, given how often we were fucking at the cabin and that I missed a few pills. While I am trying to get on board with this, I cannot stop obsessing over the fact that we don't know whose baby it is. So, I would like to take the time to discuss this because I really need to know how everyone feels about it. And not how you think I want you to feel about it, how you *really* feel about it."

The pause in the room was more pregnant than I was as we sat there silently, looking around the table to see who was going to speak next.

"Okay. I'll go first," Alex offered. "I have said from the very start that the only thing that mattered to me was

Georgia and making sure she was happy. I have always wanted kids and a big family, so I'm thrilled that she's going to have a baby."

"I never thought about settling down and having kids," Dex admitted quietly, looking at the table before lifting his eyes to meet mine. "But the thought that Georgia might be carrying my child has changed something deep inside of me. I mean, I was willing to fight an old lady this morning for the last of the maple donuts."

I pressed my lips together to keep from laughing, but it did nothing to hide the grin on my face.

"But, even if the baby *isn't* mine," Dex continued. "I am still thrilled that I get to be an uncle. Either way, I already love this baby, and there's literally nothing that will change that."

I looked away, trying to hide the tears that were forming in my eyes.

"I feel the same way," Alex said, squeezing my hand to get my attention. "I love this baby regardless of who the father is. This baby is our baby, all three of us. We're going to love it more than anyone has ever loved a baby before."

I tipped my head forward and let the tears flow freely down my cheeks. I had no idea what I ever did to deserve a love like this.

Thirty-Seven

Alex

I knew that Georgia was having a hard time wrapping her head around everything now that we knew she was pregnant. Hell, I would be lying if I said it hadn't been weighing on my mind as well. While she was stressed about not knowing who the father was, I was more focused on restraining myself from buying a ton of baby stuff and setting up a nursery. I was more than thrilled that we were having a baby, all three of us.

I woke up early on Christmas morning and snuck out of bed to surprise Georgia with her favorite breakfast. I knew Dex would be over in a bit to spend the day with us, just like we always did every year on Christmas. I loved that nothing had changed other than Georgia being pregnant.

I flipped the pancakes and then pulled the bacon from the other skillet, setting them on a paper towel before removing the pancakes.

"I thought I smelled something cooking," Georgia said as she walked into the kitchen and rubbed the sleep from her eyes. "It smells delicious."

"Perfect timing. Everything is ready, though I was going to bring you breakfast in bed."

"I can go back to bed if you want?" she offered with the cutest smile. "Or I can sit on your lap and eat like I did at the cabin."

My cock immediately twitched at the memory.

"Maybe if you're a good girl and eat all of your breakfast, I'll eat *you* when we're done," I said, pulling her into me as I nipped at her neck.

"We get to eat Georgia for breakfast?" Dex said, walking in with a grin.

He'd had a key for as long as I could remember, and I was glad he used it instead of worrying about intruding. Our home was his home, and I wanted him to always feel welcomed here.

"That's the plan," I said with a wink as Georgia pulled away, her cheeks filled with color.

"Good morning, Dex," she said, turning to accept the hug he offered.

"Good morning, beautiful. Merry Christmas," he replied as he pressed a kiss to her forehead and rested his hand on her stomach.

I thought I was obsessed with Georgia being pregnant, but it seemed Dex was just as obsessed as I was. We hadn't had sex since we found out a few days ago, but I had a feeling that was all about to change soon by the heated glances that were happening around me.

"Merry Christmas," Georgia said, smiling at both of us. "I think the best gift is going to be that heavenly food Alex made, if he will ever give it to me."

She chewed her lip playfully, her bratty side starting to come out.

"I'll make you a plate if you want to sit down and get comfortable."

She smiled at me and scrunched her nose before heading to the living room and taking her seat on the couch. We were anything but formal here, so most of our meals were eaten on the couch while we watched TV or listened to music.

"Do you need help?" Dex offered as he rubbed his hands together.

"Na, everything is done. Go ahead and make your plate, and I'll put on a pot of coffee for us."

I finished plating Georgia's food and then took it to her.

"What would you like to drink, my love?"

She worried her lip between her teeth as she thought about it.

"Orange juice sounds good," she replied, but I could hear it in her voice that she didn't really want it.

"Are you sure? It doesn't really sound like it."

"Well, I really want a cup of coffee, but I know I shouldn't drink caffeine while pregnant."

"You can have a cup a day and it won't affect the baby," Dex said as he joined us with his plate full of food.

"How do you know that?" Georgia asked with a cute grin.

"It's in the baby book I'm reading."

"You're reading a baby book?" Her eyes widened as her eyebrows rose to the top of her head.

"Yeah. Once I knew you were pregnant, I bought a couple. I wanted to know as much as I could about it so I could help out and support you." He shrugged his shoulders as if it were no big deal, but I could tell by the tears dotting Georgia's eyes that it was a huge deal for her.

"Dex," she whispered, shaking her head as if that would keep the tears from falling. "You didn't have to do that."

"I don't have to do a lot of things, Georgia. I wanted to. This baby means a lot to me, and I want to be there for you. For all of us."

"That's really cool," I said, nodding my head. "I read the same thing, that you can have a cup of coffee per day without hurting the baby."

"You're reading baby books, too?" Georgia asked, turning her head to me in surprise.

"No, I don't have any books. I've been using a few apps and looking up information online."

"I can't believe you two," she said with a sniffle. "That is so amazing. Now I feel like a terrible mother because I haven't read a single thing about being pregnant or what to do once the baby gets here."

"You're far from a terrible mother," I assured her as I kneeled beside her on the floor. "Georgia, you've known you were pregnant for a few days. Give yourself some grace, there's a lot going on, and Dex and I want to make sure we can support you however you need."

She nodded and wiped the tears from her cheeks with the back of her hand.

"Thank you. You guys seriously are the best."

"Eat your breakfast and feed that little baby of ours," I said playfully as I stood up and kissed the top of her head.

She let out the cutest giggle and then started eating while I went back to the kitchen to make some coffee and fix my food. I loved that Dex really was as invested in this as I was. It warmed my heart to see the love he had for my wife and the baby already.

Thirty-Eight
Dex

"This is by far my favorite gift so far," I said as I leaned in and slid my tongue along Georgia's thigh as she shivered beneath me. I gently pressed my hands down on her thighs to open her up and grinned when I saw her pussy glistening with arousal.

"Even more than the new sweater I got you?" Georgia teased, looking down at me as she propped herself up on her elbows.

"Baby, I will wear that sweater while I devour your pussy. But yes, eating you out is always the best gift. Now, be a good girl and lie down so I can get started. You know I'm not a patient man," I warned, my cock hardening as I leaned in and swiped my tongue along her slit.

She hissed as her hands dug into the sheet beside me, as my tongue parted her and slid inside of her pussy.

"Fuck! Dex!" she cried out, spurring me to suck her clit hard.

"You always look so beautiful with Dex in between your legs, baby," Alex said, sitting on the bed beside her.

It was hard trying to fit all of us on their king-sized bed after having the comfort of the giant bed at the cabin. But this worked, nonetheless.

I could feel her tightening around my mouth already, so I pulled away and slid a finger inside of her instead.

"Dex," she groaned in frustration, but I didn't want her to come just yet. I wanted her to come long and hard, the way I knew she could. "I was already so close."

"I know, baby, and I had barely touched you. I want you to come when I tell you to, so you're going to have to wait."

"Fucker," she muttered as Alex and I both chuckled.

I inserted another finger inside of her and stimulated her G-spot while Alex leaned over and caressed her breasts before pulling a puckered nipple into his mouth. I brushed my thumb against her clit, grinning when she bucked beneath my touch, her hips immediately lifting. She panted heavily as Alex continued torturing her nipples, taking turns with each one while I worked her G-spot.

She whimpered and squirmed, trying to get more friction against her clit, but I wanted her to squirt instead. I pressed my hand down gently on her lower stomach, then immediately removed it when I realized I might hurt the baby. Fuck, I hadn't thought about what changes we would need to make as far as sex went with Georgia now that she was pregnant. My mind started spinning as I worried that I was going to accidentally poke the baby with my finger while trying to get Georgia off.

"You're fine," Alex said, pulling his mouth away from her breast to look at me. "You're not going to hurt the baby."

A burst of air rushed out of me as I nodded, thankful that he had at least read about that since I hadn't.

"I swear to God, if you don't keep doing what you were doing, I'm going to lose my mind, Dex," Georgia warned with her eyes closed. "I am so fucking close, you better not deprive me of this one."

I laughed and shook my head, letting all of the fear go as I resumed what I was doing and put gentle pressure on her lower stomach while I worked her G-spot.

Her climax was almost instantaneous as a stream of fluid came out of her, soaking my hand as she spasmed around it.

"I fucking love it when she squirts," Alex said, looking down at the wet spot beneath her.

"Me too."

"Me three," Georgia said, looking up at both of us. "But I really love when both of you fuck me at the same time, so if we're still giving gifts and all…"

"I am in the giving mood," Alex teased with a wink.

"Just call me Santa because I'll deliver *all* the gifts," I added. "However, I think I want to use the new toy you got from Alex instead. Maybe he can fuck you while I use it on you."

Georgia's cheeks flushed a deep crimson as she looked at Alex.

"I think it's a fucking hot idea," he agreed.

I climbed off the bed to get the toy while Alex helped Georgia clean up. When I returned, Alex was lying on the bed as he helped Georgia straddle him in reverse cowgirl position. I loved how gorgeous she looked with her breasts on full display and her legs spread as she lowered herself onto his cock.

"Fuck, Georgia," I said with a heavy sigh, my cock aching to be inside of her.

While I knew some things were safe during pregnancy, I wasn't sure that her taking both of us at the same time was a good idea.

"You feel larger than usual," she whimpered over her shoulder to Alex.

"Yeah, you're super tight, baby. Try to relax, my love. I don't want this to hurt you."

She nodded, but I could see the hesitation as she struggled to slide the rest of the way down his cock. I knew she had been aroused a few minutes ago, but I didn't know if maybe something about being pregnant made it harder for her to stay aroused. I set the toy down on the nightstand and slowly climbed on the bed, licking my lips as I kneeled in front of her.

"You take his cock so well, baby," I said softly, knowing how much my dirty words usually turned her on. "Look at how tight your pussy is gripping it. So fucking hot, Georgia."

I leaned in and slid my hand around the back of her neck as I brought my lips to hers and gently kissed her. Alex waited patiently with his hands on her hips as my tongue explored her mouth. My hands skimmed her waist before moving up to cup her breasts.

Her hands slowly dipped below my waist and cupped my erection through the sweats I had on. I groaned into the kiss, loving how quickly she had my cock out and was stroking it without any mercy. She pulled away, breaking the kiss as she looked at me with heated desire.

"I want to suck your cock," she breathed, her body relaxing enough to allow her to sink lower on Alex's cock.

"Fuck, Georgia," I said, shoving a hand through my hair.

"Can I?"

"I don't think we can really do it in this position," I admitted. Not only that, but I wanted to make sure she got off from the toy.

"If you stand up, you should be right in line with my face," she said softly as she chewed her lip.

"I don't want to risk falling on you, baby."

"If Georgia leans forward, I can shift us so she's on her hands and knees while I take her from behind," Alex offered. "You can lie on the bed while she takes your cock in her mouth."

"That would work," Georgia said happily.

"Are you sure?"

She nodded at the same time Alex did. I climbed off the bed to get undressed while they switched position. Alex had pulled them toward the headboard, leaving plenty of room for me to lie down at the foot of the bed. It felt weird to be sideways, but I didn't care about anything the second Georgia lowered herself above my cock and slowly licked the tip of it. I closed my eyes and felt my cock harden as she swirled her tongue around, consuming the drop of precum in the process.

The bed shook as Alex began thrusting inside of her, but Georgia didn't seem bothered as she took me deep into the back of her throat. I smoothed my hand down her back as she hollowed her cheeks and sucked harder. I was going to come in a matter of seconds at this rate.

"Fuck, that view is so hot. We should do this all the time. I love watching you suck Dex's cock as I fuck this tight pussy of yours, baby," Alex said.

Georgia moaned in response, her hand gripping my shaft tightly as she stroked what didn't fit in her mouth.

"Baby, I'm going to come," I warned, my body stiffening in response.

I looked at her face and found a devious smile as she pulled my cock out of her mouth, teased it with her tongue, then took it straight to the back of her throat again. I wanted to keep my eyes open and watch her, but the pleasure was so intense that they tightened shut as I shot ropes of cum down her throat.

Once I was done, she slowly pulled herself off my cock and wiped the corners of her lips. She winked at me as if she didn't know what that fucking did to me. My body felt drained and thoroughly satisfied, but I was still determined to make Georgia come again.

I carefully climbed over to the other side of the bed and grabbed the candy cane shaped vibrator from the nightstand. Alex grinned and adjusted his position as he held onto her. I sat as close as I could without getting in the way and turned on the toy.

Georgia's eyes shot open as soon as she heard the sound and studied it.

"It seems fitting to use the candy cane vibrator on you since it's Christmas," I said with a grin.

I knew that Alex had bought her a handful of toys from Dark Vibes before he knew she was pregnant. It was something they used often in the bedroom, so it wasn't a surprise that he would get her new ones. But seeing one that looked just like a candy cane impressed me.

 Georgia's cheeks split into a grin as she watched me slide the toy between them and then gasped as it made contact with her clit.

"I want you to come hard for us, baby," I said, pressing it directly against her clit.

"Ahhh," she cried out. "It's too much. Too much."

I pulled it away and changed the setting to a lower speed, and then slowly pressed it against her clit again.

"Better?"

She nodded, her eyes closed as she breathed heavily.

"Fuck. I can feel that on my dick," Alex said, gripping her hips tighter.

I adjusted the toy so the short side of the candy cane pressed against her clit and the curve of it touched his cock.

Alex grunted and came inside Georgia at the same time she cried out, coming on the toy. As soon as she was finished, I pulled the toy away and rolled to the other side of the bed, where we all collapsed in a pile of satisfied bliss.

Thirty-Nine

Georgia

It was mid-January by the time I was able to get an appointment with my OBGYN. While that would have typically stressed me out, I found myself more relaxed with all of the information the guys had given me about pregnancy. Every day, Alex would tell me something new about the changes that were happening with my body that he learned from his app, while Dex would update us on what he was learning in the books he was reading. It was like we were one big, happy family that was embarking on the journey of parenthood together.

I sat on the exam table with a cloth draped over my legs, waiting for the doctor to come in as Alex sat beside me, squeezing my hand. It felt weird to be there without Dex, but I wasn't ready to explain that relationship to anyone just yet. My main priority was making sure the baby was okay.

A knock on the door startled me out of my thoughts as it pushed open, as the doctor came into the room.

"Sorry for the delay today, we're running a little behind," she said as she smiled at both of us and took a seat in front of the computer that sat on the small desk beside the exam table.

"No worries," I replied, my leg beginning to bounce before Alex gently placed his hand on it to stop it.

"I see in the notes that you're pregnant. Congratulations," she said, turning to face us.

"Thank you," we replied at the same time.

"I don't know how far along I am," I stammered, not sure why I felt the need to admit that.

"Not a problem. We can do an ultrasound and compare it to the date of your last period to get a better idea of when you conceived."

I nodded and took a deep breath in, holding it a little too long before exhaling heavily.

"So, as the nurse might have explained, this early in the pregnancy, we have to do a transvaginal ultrasound," the doctor said as she got everything ready and turned to face me. "When you're ready, I will have you insert the wand, and then I'll take it from there."

Alex looked away as I took it from her under the sheet and did as she asked. Once she took over, I laid back and closed my eyes, feeling a bit embarrassed.

"Alright, let's take a look," she said softly, as I felt it move inside of me. "Here is your bab—"

My eyes flew open, and I stiffened as I heard the pause in her voice.

"What's wrong?" I asked, immediately scared that something had happened.

"Nothing. Nothing at all," she reassured me with a genuine smile. "I'm sorry. What I meant to say is here are your *babies*."

She pointed to the image on the screen with her free hand, moving from one bean-looking thing to another. Alex lifted his phone and pretended to be checking something, but I knew he was really getting photos and video to show Dex later. He had to be discreet since we knew we weren't supposed to do that.

"*Babies*?" I clarified, staring in disbelief.

"Yes. You are carrying twins."

"Holy shit," Alex said beside me as he leaned forward to get a better view.

"I would say, based on the size of the embryos and the date of your last period, that you are around seven or eight weeks pregnant. Do you want to hear the heartbeats?"

"Yes, please," Alex rushed out, squeezing my hand as we both stared at the monitor at the two tiny embryos.

The doctor grinned as she turned up the volume and held the wand in one spot, the sound echoing in the room as the baby's heart beat fast and steady. She then moved the wand, and the sound played again.

"They both have strong heartbeats," she said, grinning at us.

"That's amazing," Alex said, completely mesmerized.

I nodded, but the words wouldn't come out as they got stuck in my throat.

I wasn't just pregnant and didn't know who the father was.

I was pregnant with twins.

Forty

Dex

"Twins?" I asked in disbelief as I looked back and forth between Georgia and Alex.

"Yep. Twins," Alex confirmed as he grinned at Georgia.

"As in *two* babies?" I clarified, the thought of Georgia carrying twins was messing with my head in a way I hadn't anticipated.

"That's usually what it means," Alex replied with a playful laugh.

"How do you feel about this?" I asked Georgia, turning my attention directly to her.

She shrugged and let her shoulders fall as she exhaled heavily.

"I was just getting used to the idea that I was pregnant. But now I'm going to have two babies and I'm a little terrified."

"I told you, baby. It's going to be alright. This isn't anything we can't handle." Alex rubbed her back soothingly.

"How is it going to be alright? I can't take care of two babies by myself."

"Why would you be taking care of them by yourself?" I questioned, wondering what had happened during her doctor's appointment to make her feel that way.

"I mean, I wouldn't be by myself *all* the time. But I would be by myself while Alex is at work."

Alex. Not both of us, just Alex.

I tried not to let it bother me that she hadn't included me in that statement because I knew that at the end of the day, he was still her husband and I wasn't. Even though we had this arrangement when it came to sex, none of us had talked about what the plans would be if she got pregnant. While we all agreed that we were on board with the three of us doing this together, I couldn't blame her for only looking at this as something she and Alex would have to worry about.

"You will have my support the entire time, baby. We'll have Dex as well. He's as involved in all of this as we are. So, if you really think about it, the babies will be outnumbered. We got this."

"I'm sorry. I didn't mean to exclude you, Dex," Georgia said, looking up at me with such sadness in her eyes.

"It's fine, I get it."

"What's that supposed to mean?" Alex asked, immediately calling me out.

"It means that I get that this is bigger than any of us have ever planned for. You guys are husband and wife. I'm just the friend who gets to play and have fun. I don't blame

Georgia for thinking about this as something that she's sharing with her husband."

"Yeah, and we also talked about how we'd all be involved regardless," Alex countered.

"I know," I said, sighing heavily. "I'm not saying that I don't want to be involved. I'm just saying that I understand that there might be a time when I need to step back and just be the… uncle." I threw my hands in the air, frustrated that my words felt like they were getting jumbled in my head and not coming out the way I wanted them to.

"I don't think we need to worry about any of that right now," Georgia said, interrupting us. "We have plenty of time to figure all of that out. There are bigger things that I would rather deal with now that we know there are two babies."

"Absolutely, baby," Alex said, standing behind her and wrapping his arms around her waist. "What is weighing on your mind, my love?"

"This house. I love this house and I know that we've lived here forever, but I don't know how we're supposed to fit two babies when we barely have enough room for the two of us. We have one bathroom. One extra bedroom. No backyard. I just…" She blew out a breath and let her shoulders fall. "I don't know how to make more room, but I know we need to figure out a way. I can sell my books and get rid of the bookshelves in the guest room so we can turn it into a nursery."

"No, absolutely not," Alex and I said at the same time.

"You're not getting rid of your books," Alex replied softly.

"We don't have the room, Alex. It's either five bookshelves filled with books I've already read, or cribs and changing tables and toys galore. But we can't have both."

"Okay, so we'll look at buying a new house."

"What?" She turned and faced him. "We can't just buy a new house. We have babies on the way."

"We can, and you're right, we don't have enough room here for everyone. It makes sense that we need a bigger house."

"Houses cost money, as do babies. We can't just go around blowing money we don't have. And what if we don't find a house that fits what we want? You and I both know that there's not a ton of houses for sale around here, and the ones that are up for sale are old and need a ton of repairs."

"Okay, then I'll build us one." Alex grinned widely as Georgia's eyebrows rose.

"You can't just build us a house," she said with a laugh.

"Why not? Believe it or not, Dex and I know how to build houses."

She turned and looked at me, almost as if she had forgotten I was still there. I folded my arms over my chest and nodded.

"Baby, I love you. And I love that you want to do whatever you can to make me happy, but this is a little extreme," she said softly as she brushed her thumb over her cheek. "We don't have the money to just go build a house."

"Georgia, you forget that I work for fun. Well, that and to keep Dex from getting in trouble. We have more than enough in our savings that I could retire today and we would still be set for the rest of our lives. If you want your dream house, we will build it for you. Exactly how you want it."

I knew that Alex had a trust fund when we met in college, but he never talked about how much was in it. It didn't surprise me that Georgia didn't seem to know how much money they had, either, given she was never the kind to ask for anything and liked to live a simple life. She didn't want or need fancy or expensive things and much preferred a simple, clean environment free from clutter.

"So, what do you say, baby. Can we build you the house of your dreams?" Alex asked, lifting her chin so she would look at him.

"If you're busy building our house, then what does that mean for Dex? He won't be able to work other jobs if he's helping you."

"I'll be fine," I said, not wanting to elaborate on how I had a hefty savings account of my own.

"I don't like that at all. You have a mortgage and a car payment," Georgia objected, turning to face me.

"Technically, my truck is paid off." I paused and watched the surprise flash across her face. "So is my house."

"What?" She covered her mouth and giggled as she stared at me with bewilderment. "Are you serious?"

I nodded, loving how cute she looked.

"Yeah, I don't need to work either. I just do it because it's fun and I get to hang out with Alex."

"All this time I thought you two worked because you needed the money like regular people," she replied with a shake of her head and a laugh.

"Nope. We are fortunate to have the luxury of not working if we don't want to. Which also means that once we get the house built and you have the babies, we can both be home with you to help take care of them," Alex said.

Georgia glanced at me and then at Alex before she spoke.

"I might be out of line here because I know we haven't discussed it," Georgia said nervously. "But if Dex is going to be here helping out with the babies and helping to build our dream house, it seems only fitting that he live with us. I don't want to make you uncomfortable by asking, but it just doesn't feel like it will be our home without you there. Like all the time there, not just visiting. Kinda like we had at the cabin."

Alex smiled and leaned down to kiss the top of her head.

"I was actually just thinking the same thing," he said. "We had a great time at the cabin, and we got along just fine while we were stuck up there. You're family and it's not like you won't be here all the time anyway."

I licked my lips then pulled in a sharp breath as I considered my answer.

"Are you guys sure about this?"

They both nodded while Georgia held her hands in front of her and waited.

"Yeah, I'll move into the new house with you guys when it's ready," I said, grinning when Georgia rushed over and threw her arms around my neck.

"Or, you can move into this one *now*," Alex said, smirking.

Georgia's head whipped around to stare at him before turning back to me.

"I don't want to make anyone uncomfortable," I stammered. It was a stupid lie, but I didn't want to spring anything on Georgia without giving her time to process it. Moving into the house they were building meant she had months to get used to the idea. Moving into their current house gave her no time at all to adjust to having me live with them.

"Why would anyone be uncomfortable?" she asked with a hint of hurt in her voice.

"I don't know. I just… I…" I pressed my lips together as I tried to figure out what I wanted to say. "I care about you so much, Georgia. I don't want to do anything to hurt you or make you feel uncomfortable. If it were up to me, I would move in today and spend the money to buy a giant bed to replace the one in the bedroom so we could all share it like we did at the cabin. I would do whatever I could to help with things around here. But I don't want to rush you into something if you need a little more time."

She looked over her shoulder at Alex and then back to me, this time wearing a mischievous grin.

"Well, then, I guess it's a good thing that it is up to you. I'm going to go rearrange some stuff in the closet so we have room for your clothes while you and Alex start packing your stuff."

She leaned up and kissed my lips, making me want to do more than just kiss her right now.

I looked at Alex when she pulled away, trying to get a feel for how he felt about everything.

"Let's get going. We have a lot to pack up," he said, walking over and patting my shoulder before heading to the kitchen.

I stood there for a minute, completely shocked by what happened. In less than thirty minutes, I found out Georgia was carrying twins and that I was moving into their house. Talk about embracing the unexpected.

Forty-One
Georgia

I spent the day going through our bedroom closet to make room for Dex's stuff. While we had the guest room, there wasn't any space in the closet because that was where I stored boxes of craft stuff and decorations, given that we didn't have a garage. Our house had always fit what Alex and I needed, but now that our family was growing, we needed much more space.

I never made it a priority to know exactly how much money we had, since Alex took care of everything and paid all our bills. I knew when I met him that he had money set aside from a trust fund, but I didn't care to know how much it was. I was in love with him and wanted to spend the rest of my life with him, regardless of how much money he had.

When he proposed building our own house, I went through a flurry of emotions. It felt so unrealistic and surreal that it was even a possibility. But then seeing both him and Dex on board with making it happen made my heart swell more than I could have imagined. The thought of having Dex live with us forever was something I had secretly been thinking about, but I never imagined it would be something that came true.

"Hey, baby. We're back," Alex called from the kitchen.

I set down the pile of clothes that I was going through and headed out there to see them.

"That was quick," I said, wrapping my arms around his neck to hug him as I glanced at the clock.

"We didn't get everything today. Just the essentials for now," Alex said after kissing me.

I could tell there was something he wasn't saying, but I didn't want to push him, so I let it go.

"Sounds good. I was just finishing up in the room, and then I'll start dinner. I made some space for his stuff in the closet."

"You didn't have to do that," Dex said, coming in and setting a duffel bag down on the kitchen table.

"I wanted to. If you're going to live here, you need space too."

"Yeah, but I don't need much. I don't want you overdoing it," he objected.

"I'm fine. I promise. Aside from being a little nauseous, I'm good. The doctor said I don't have to change anything that I'm doing."

"How about you finish what you have going on in the bedroom, and I will start dinner," Alex offered, his hands gripping my waist.

Before I could say anything, Dex stepped beside us and gave me a look.

"I'll go help Georgia in the bedroom, and then we'll come help you with dinner."

"I don't need any help, I've g—"

Dex lifted his finger and pressed it against my lips.

"If I'm going to live here, you're going to let me help with stuff. Starting with whatever project you have going in the bedroom."

He pulled his finger away, but I could feel the sexual tension crackle in the air around us from his touch.

"Did you just cut me off and boss me around?" I asked, narrowing my eyes as I planted a hand on my hip and stared at him.

He straightened his back and tilted his head as he looked down at me with one eyebrow arched.

Fuck. He was so sexy. This bossy side of him always did stuff to me.

"Are you talking back to me right now?"

"Are you trying to play a power move with *me* right now?" I put both hands on my hips, trying to appear tougher.

He chewed his lower lip as he made a tsking sound. Before I could process what was happening, he picked me up, tossed me over his shoulder, and spanked my ass as he stormed down the hallway to the bedroom while Alex laughed in the kitchen.

It was in that moment that I realized just how fun it was going to be having Dex live with us.

<u>Forty-Two</u>

Alex

Six-ish Months Later

"What do you think?" I asked Georgia as she walked through the empty living room of our new house, loving the waddle in her steps.

"It's great," she said as she tugged at her shirt that was pulled tight over her swollen stomach.

"Just great?" I tilted my head and studied her, trying to figure out what it was that she didn't like.

We'd spent months going over the blueprint and layout for the new house with all of us giving input on what we wanted. Georgia insisted on an open-concept design for the living room and kitchen, with a small room off to the side where the babies could play when they got older.

The idea was to set up the room with a table in the middle, with cubbies and bins along the wall to store their stuff. She wanted to have an art station set up where they could explore their creativity in a space that was safe to do so while being out of the way.

She also insisted on giving Dex his own room, just in case anything changed and he needed space of his own. Which seemed odd, given that he had already been living with us for a few months and there hadn't been any problems. He objected several times, but we all conceded when she cried for an hour nonstop over it. While we knew the hormones were to blame, that didn't make us feel any better about making her cry.

"No, it's amazing. It's everything I pictured when we started planning it," she said with a sigh as her shoulders shrugged.

"What's wrong, baby?" I held her in front of me and wrapped my hands around her waist as I looked at her beautiful face.

"Nothing. I'm just uncomfortable, and nothing fits anymore."

"Well, you are seven months pregnant, my love."

"Yeah. Most women have cute little baby bumps. I look like I swallowed a whale. My stomach is so big, I can't even see my feet anymore."

"That's because you're carrying twins," Dex said, coming around the corner and smiling at her before placing a kiss on her cheek and rubbing his hand across her stomach. "But if you need new clothes, let's go buy some today. I'll do laundry tonight so you have them for tomorrow."

"I just bought new clothes," Georgia whined, but I understood her frustration. Her body was changing quickly, and while I loved the new curves and the roundness of her stomach, I knew she was constantly feeling uncomfortable and miserable with everything fitting tighter, especially in this summer heat.

"Yeah, but if they don't fit comfortably, then we should get you stuff that fits better," Dex replied softly, his hand still on her belly. "Or, you can go naked. I like that idea better."

The corners of her mouth turned up as she tried to fight a smile.

"You're the worst," she teased.

"Na, baby. I'm the best. I proved that last night when you came on my tongue while reading your book."

I laughed, very clearly remembering the image of Dex between her legs on the floor while she sat on the couch and devoured another book in the Beaumont Creek series that she loved so much. I sat there and watched, jerking myself off when I knew she was too tired for all of us to play the way we wanted to.

Georgia shook her head and tried to hide a yawn behind her hand, but we both saw it.

"Alright. I think we're done here," I said, rubbing my hand up and down her back. "Why don't we head home and I'll fix something for dinner while you rest."

"I'm fine," she objected as another yawn slipped out. "I didn't sleep well last night, but then again, I don't sleep well most nights these days. It's like an inferno in our bedroom."

"I'm sorry, baby. This heatwave has been miserable for everyone. But the good news is that we can start moving stuff in here this weekend, so at least we will have refrigerated air to help keep the house cool," I replied.

"That sounds heavenly." She smiled so big that it wrinkled the sides of her eyes, and it made my heart swell. I loved seeing Georgia happy, and I wasn't lying when I told her we would do everything we could to keep her comfortable during her pregnancy, even if that meant working non-stop on the house every day like we had been for the past few months.

"Let's head home, have some dinner, and then I'll check online for an update on when the bed will be delivered," Dex said, winking at Georgia. "We can't move in until we have the proper bed."

"I will sleep on the floor if it means I have refrigerated air," Georgia said tightly.

"Over my dead body," Dex replied, standing next to her and starting the stare down that usually ended with him fixing her attitude.

"I love you, but I'm not above making that happen." She stared into his eyes, holding his gaze as he tried not to smile. "Hell, I might even use your dead body to sleep on in my new house with refrigerated air."

Dex's eyebrows rose and he looked past her to me, looking slightly worried. I lifted my hands and shook my head. There was no way I was getting in the middle of this.

"I don't recall reading anything in those pregnancy books about violence and murder," he teased.

"It's in the chapter called fuck around and find out. It happens during the seventh month of pregnancy for mothers carrying twins. It's usually triggered by heat and an inability to get comfortable," Georgia said as she turned and walked away. "Come on, let's go. That house isn't going to pack itself."

I shook my head and laughed. There was no stopping Georgia once she had her mind set on something.

Forty-Three
Georgia

I laid spread out on our new Alaskan King bed, enjoying the cold refrigerated air. It only took the guys two days to get the majority of our stuff moved into the new house, and I hadn't been happier. Once the bed was delivered, it was all green flags and no stopping from there. They even had a few guys they had worked with before who volunteered to help move everything over while I took care of making things look nice. So far, that included fluffing the new pillows on the couch and arranging the flowers the guys bought me this morning to celebrate our first day living in our new house.

The smell of hamburgers floated through the air, immediately making me get off the bed and head in the direction of the savory food. I was constantly hungry these days, but I did my best to stick to a healthy diet. But, I also wasn't one to turn down one of Alex's signature bacon cheeseburgers with sweet potato fries.

I walked through the house, loving the feel of the new carpet beneath my bare feet. The walls were all painted a pretty cream color that complemented the brand-new gray furniture we had chosen as a team. I wanted Dex to be as involved in everything as Alex and I were, but I did have to stop him when he tried to buy a sex swing and a Tantra chair because I didn't want to have to someday explain those items to our children. It would be challenging enough to explain our relationship and why the three of us shared a bedroom, but that would be an obstacle to face another day. For now, I was only concerned with making sure the twins had everything they needed and knew how loved they were by the three of us.

I looked outside and grinned when I found both of them standing at the grill, drinking beer, and laughing about something. I loved having Dex around all the time, and that it just felt right for him to be so involved in our lives. I opened the door and stepped outside, lifting my hand to shield my eyes from the sun.

"Hey, beautiful," Dex said, pulling me into his side as he blocked the sun for me. "How are you feeling?"

"Good. The nap helped, even if I didn't want to take it," I admitted, putting a hand over my stomach as one of the babies kicked.

"I'm glad. Dinner will be ready soon."

"I could smell it in the bedroom, so I came in search of food."

Just then, an intense pain spread across my stomach that made me gasp and bend over. I scrunched my face and tried to breathe through it as my entire stomach felt like it was tightening.

"Whoa, are you okay?" Alex said, setting his beer down and stepping toward me.

I nodded, unable to answer as I felt both of them watching me intently.

"Yeah," I replied with a soft laugh, trying to brush it off. "I guess these babies are just hungry. Talk about hunger pains."

A few minutes passed, but neither of them laughed as I noticed the concern etched on their faces. Before I could try to convince them I was okay, another one hit.

"Shit. She's having contractions," Dex said, setting his beer down and holding onto my other elbow to steady me while Alex grabbed the other side.

"They're probably just Braxton hicks," I offered, knowing that the doctor said to come in if I started having any contractions. Things were different when you were carrying twins, especially for a woman my age.

"We're not taking any chances," Alex said, looking around me to see Dex. "I've got her if you want to go grab the hospital bag and load it into the car. I'll turn the grill off and we'll head out."

"What? I don't get to eat first?" I asked in utter disbelief as I looked between them. "No. I demand that we stay until I've had my burger and sweet pota—"

My words were cut off with a groan as another contraction happened. Fuck. These were happening back-to-back with very little time in between. I knew that wasn't a good sign, especially since I still had at least four weeks before it would be safe to deliver.

"I will make you as many burgers as you want later. Right now, we're going to the hospital." Alex nodded at Dex, who took off sprinting through the house as if this were an emergency. Which, okay, yeah, it could be.

I blew out a breath of frustration and allowed Alex to lead me into the house before he rushed outside and turned the grill off. A few minutes later, Dex had the car packed and Alex had the house locked up as they guided me to the car.

The drive to the hospital was quick, which I appreciated, even though the contractions had stopped as soon as I got in the car. I didn't have to do much once we got there, as Dex took care of everything by rushing inside and coming back with a handful of nurses who helped me into the wheelchair and took me back to an exam room.

We had been there for half an hour with several nurses coming and going from my room as they monitored the babies. I tried to rest and relax, but it was nearly impossible with how much tension was radiating from the guys.

A few minutes later, there was a knock on the door and then my doctor appeared.

"How are we feeling?" she asked, looking at me and then immediately checking the monitor and strip of paper that kept printing. Her eyebrows rose, and then she let her shoulders fall before she turned and studied me.

"Much better. The contractions stopped before we got here. I thought I felt one or two since we've been here, but that might have just been hunger pains because *someone* wouldn't let me eat before we came," I answered, making a point to glare at Alex for not feeding me.

"You have had a few since you've been here, but they're not consistent, so I feel comfortable saying you're not in true labor just yet," she said with a heavy sigh. "You're thirty-one weeks, but ideally, we want to keep them in as long as possible. It's safer to deliver at thirty-five weeks if we can."

"What do we do?" Alex asked, stepping closer with his arms crossed over his chest. I'd never seen him so worried before in my life.

"There is the option to give medicine to stop the contractions and hopefully delay preterm labor. However, there are health risks that we have to take into consideration."

"Like what?" Dex asked, standing beside Alex.

"For starters, cardiovascular complications. Given that Georgia is carrying two babies, that already puts stress on her heart. Giving her tocolytics to stop the contractions can cause her to have tachycardia and hypotension, things that we would need to monitor very closely. In addition to that, there is also the risk of pulmonary edema, which is fluid accumulation in the lungs," the doctor explained.

"And if I don't take them?" I asked, wanting to know all of the options. While I knew the guys would do everything in their power to protect me, I was going to do everything in mine to protect these babies.

"If you don't take them, you may continue to go into preterm labor. If the babies are born early without any intervention, they may need additional care in the NICU. Geriatric pregnancies with twins are always high-risk pregnancies. We want to do everything we can to keep everyone healthy."

"Will the medicine hurt the babies?" Alex questioned, his face draining of color.

"Right now, everything can have an impact on them. However, if we give Georgia the tocolytic medications to slow her contractions, we will also administer corticosteroids to help develop the babies' lungs and brains. She would be admitted to the hospital, where we would monitor her and the babies while she is on bed rest," the doctor answered.

"So, what you're saying is that Georgia could suffer complications if she takes the medication?" Dex asked, his voice changing to an angry tone I hadn't heard before.

"Yes. It is one of the risks." The doctor's face was solemn as if she knew that none of the answers she gave us would be what we wanted to hear. "I will give you some privacy to discuss the information you've been given."

She turned and walked out of the room, closing the door behind her.

I sat there anxiously waiting for one of them to speak, to break the tension that was mounting in the room.

"I don't think you should take the medication," Dex said, looking at me.

"Why not?" Alex demanded, turning to face him.

"Because the risks to Georgia are high!"

"So are the risks to the babies if they are born preterm," Alex countered.

"I understand that. I'm not saying that I'm not worried about the babies. I'm saying that I'm worried that trying to stop preterm labor could kill Georgia."

"No one said I could die," I objected, desperate to change the energy in the room.

"She quite literally said just that," Dex argued. "You could get fluid in your lungs. You could experience low blood pressure and a racing heartbeat, Georgia. That's stress that your body doesn't need right now."

"But she also said that they would monitor her constantly," Alex said, his face slightly red with anger. "They would monitor her *and* the babies to make sure everyone is okay."

"And what if she's not okay? What if we lose her because we decide it's best to stop early labor? Shouldn't we expect that her body knows what it needs, and if labor is going to start early, it's for a reason?"

"No! Women go into preterm labor all the time, Dex. You know that. We read about it in all of the books. Preterm labor doesn't have to be a death sentence," Alex objected. "I think the best option for everyone is to start the medications to try to stop early labor."

"I disagree," Dex argued, folding his arms tighter over his chest.

"Well, I'm sorry. I feel we need to do what's best for my wife."

"*Your* wife," Dex replied, pressing his lips together as he nodded his head.

"Yes. My wife. At the end of the day, she is and always will be *my* wife. And those babies—"

"You don't even know that you're the father!" Dex roared, startling me so bad that the machine beeped as my blood pressure spiked.

They both stopped and turned to look at me as tears ran down my cheeks, and my lip trembled.

"I can clearly see my place here," Dex said quietly as he hung his head.

Then he walked over to the other side of the bed, kissed my head, and wiped a tear from my cheek.

"I love you, Georgia. I will always love you."

Then he turned around and left without looking back. And that was how we ruined the relationship that we promised would never be taken for granted. That was how our best friend walked out of our lives.

Forty-Four
Dex

It had been two weeks since I walked away from Georgia at the hospital, and I hadn't had the balls to go back. Between the missed calls from Alex and Georgia and the text messages that I left on read and never responded to, I knew that she was still in the hospital, but she and the babies were doing well.

I hadn't expected to react the way I did when Alex and I got into it at the hospital. After I got home—to my old house, not the one we'd built together—I sat down and realized what an asshole I had been all along. On top of that, I realized just how much my love for Georgia had grown because the thought of there being even a slight possibility that she wouldn't make it had me spiraling out of control.

My fear of losing her had overridden everything else, and I felt terrible that I let things get out of hand and upset her the way I had. I loved those babies and would never want anything bad to happen to them, but I also wanted them to come into a world where they got to know their mother and see what a beautiful person she was. My heart felt like it was going to explode in my chest when I thought about a world without Georgia in it.

I had been working on a few side jobs while I tried to clear my mind and distract myself. I knew that at some point, I would need to find courage and talk to both of them. But today wasn't the day. I knew that while Georgia was now thirty-three weeks pregnant, it was still risky for her to deliver the twins this early. I couldn't stand the thought of being there and possibly stressing her out with all of my worrying. So I did what I thought was best and stayed away. Alex was strong and would support her in a way I couldn't right now.

It was getting late and I was starving, but since I hadn't bothered to grocery shop in who knew how long, I ordered a pizza for delivery and jumped in the shower. Right as I got out and dressed, I heard the doorbell ring.

I opened the door and then almost immediately slammed it shut when I saw who was on the other side.

"What are you doing here?" I asked, gripping the side of the door a little too tightly.

"I came to talk to you," Alex said, his hand shoved into his pockets as he waited for me to let him inside.

I wanted to counter and tell him that I wasn't ready to talk about things yet, but I knew that if he was making an effort, I needed to as well.

"Pizza will be here soon," I replied as I stepped aside and let him in.

"I won't be here long. I want to get back to Georgia. But since you won't answer our calls or texts, I figured showing up unannounced was the only way to get through to you right now."

"How is she doing?" I asked, finding myself desperate for any information he was willing to give me.

"She's hanging in there. She's restless being cooped up in the hospital room, but she's binge-watching some home décor reality show and is obsessed with all of the things she wants to do to the house once she goes home."

I grinned because I could absolutely picture her doing this.

"How are the babies?"

"They're good. Growing and giving their mama a break. The doctor gave Georgia the medicine to stop her contractions, and thankfully, it worked. They've been monitoring her and the babies closely."

I let out a heavy breath and shoved a hand through my hair before I looked at him and shook my head.

"I'm so fucking sorry," I said, trying to ignore the emotion thick in my voice.

"Don't be. I was an asshole for pulling the husband crap. You're just as much a part of all of this as I am. I'm sorry that I made you feel like you weren't. That was super shitty of me, and I've hated myself ever since for letting it happen."

"Yeah, but you are her husband. I know we have an arrangement and whatnot, but at the end of the day, you're her husband. I can't even begin to imagine how you've felt with everything going on. I'm sorry that I wasn't there for you. I'm even more sorry that I let Georgia down by not being there for her like I promised I would."

"Well, you can start making it up to her by going back to the hospital with me," he said with a huge grin.

Just then, the doorbell rang with my pizza delivery. I opened the door and took it from the young kid before passing him a cash tip and closing the door.

"Shit. I guess I shouldn't have ordered this."

"Na. Take it with you. Georgia is cleared to have outside food and will be thrilled to have pizza."

"Really?"

"Yep. She's not showing any signs of early labor, so she's not on any restrictions other than bed rest and an IV. She's been trying to eat healthy to keep her blood pressure from getting high, but I'm sure she would love some pizza. Get whatever you need and let's go."

The tension in my shoulders lifted as I smiled back at my best friend and grabbed my phone before following him out the door and heading to see the woman we both loved.

Forty-Five
Georgia

"That pizza better be for me. If it's not, I would turn around and leave before I throw this remote at your head," I warned, knowing that Alex had snuck out for a bit earlier to run an errand but didn't say what it was. It wouldn't surprise me at all if he went out to get me my favorite food because that was just who he was.

"I see the violence hasn't stopped any," Dex said as he peeked through the door as he opened it. "Is it safe to come in, or should I send for reinforcement?"

"Do you have pizza?" I asked, ignoring the swarm of butterflies rushing through my belly at the sound of his voice.

"Yes."

"Then you may enter."

He pushed the door the rest of the way open and came inside while Alex followed behind with a goofy smile on his face.

"You brought me pizza."

I stared at him, unsure of what to say because of how things had been left between us. Not only that, he had been avoiding Alex and me for two weeks, so I had no idea where we stood.

"Technically, he had ordered it for himself, but I convinced him to bring it when I told him to get his head out of his ass and come over and fix things with you," Alex said, plopping down in the chair beside my bed.

My heart sank a little, but I tried to ignore it. Dex didn't owe me anything, especially a pizza. But that didn't dull the pain I felt when I realized that he would have been fine continuing with not speaking to us, and I hated the idea that maybe he wasn't as invested in this as I thought he was.

"Stop it," he said firmly, giving me the look that always spread fire through my belly and made me ache for him.

"Stop what?" I asked, my tone harsher than I intended.

"Stop overthinking whatever you're thinking. You're reading way too much into the whole pizza thing."

"You wouldn't have come if Alex hadn't dragged you here. You were obviously content staying home and ordering pizza and living your life free of us," I snapped, earning a sharp jab as one of the babies kicked.

He set the pizza down on the table by my bed and stood beside me as he stared into my eyes. I tried to look away, but the heat in his gaze wouldn't allow me to. I was like a moth drawn to a flame and I knew how it felt to get burned by him.

"I was an idiot, Georgia. No matter how hard I try, I will never be able to tell you how incredibly sorry I am. I let my concern for you override everything else—including logic and respect. I love you more than I have loved anyone in my life. The thought of possibly losing you made me so fucking out of my mind that I didn't know what to do. But I was an asshole about it, and for that, I'm sorry. I never meant to hurt you, and more importantly, I never should have walked away."

I scrunched my nose and turned to look away, but his fingers caught my chin and held my face in place as he continued to stare at me.

"I'm not going anywhere. I made that mistake once. I will not make it again. I am here for all of it, Georgia. There's nothing that can keep me away. I will make sure that from here on out, I do everything in my power to show you how much you and these babies mean to me," he continued.

I swallowed hard, trying to force the emotions back down. I was way too pregnant to handle any of this right now.

Alex sat beside us, completely relaxed with his hands resting on his stomach. I knew he was never one to hold grudges, so it didn't surprise me that they had already fixed whatever they needed to between them. They had been friends for so long that I couldn't imagine there would be much that would jeopardize their friendship.

Dex took a step back and continued to watch me before turning his attention to the box of pizza and the paper plates sitting on top of it. He opened the box, the smell filling the room and making my stomach growl. Then he handed me the plate and waited for me to take it.

When I hesitated, he arched an eyebrow and pinned me with a look.

"Eat," he commanded, his tone and energy shifting to the bossy one I loved best.

"Or what?" I asked, jutting my chin out.

"Oh, Georgia, Georgia, Georgia," he said with a heavy sigh before setting it down on the edge of the table closest to me. "You really don't want to do this, baby."

"How do you know what I do and don't want to do?"

What I really wanted to do was devour the entire pizza and then lick the inside of the box, but I wasn't going to tell him that.

"That attitude of yours sure does get you in trouble. And while I can't do what I want to do to you until after you have the babies, rest assured that I'll make you pay for it later."

"Promises, promises." I pulled my mouth to the side and loved the heated glance I caught before he looked away and served himself.

He sat down in the chair on the other side of my bed and leaned back, looking completely relaxed and unfazed by anything. Then he licked his lips and took a bite, letting the cheese pull as he deliberately flicked his tongue until it was in his mouth.

Fucker.

"Stop watching me and eat your pizza," he said, giving me another look that meant he was serious. "Those babies are hungry. I can hear your stomach growling from here."

I sighed heavily and then picked up the pizza and finished my slice before either of them could blink. Nothing compares to a hungry pregnant lady and pizza.

Forty-Six
Alex

"What's wrong?" I asked, scrambling awake in the chair beside Georgia as I heard her cry out in pain. Seconds later, Dex was up and standing by her side. After we made amends and everything was fine between us, he had been determined to stay at the hospital every day and every night, for the past two weeks. While Georgia had already been in the hospital for four weeks, she had reached the thirty-five-week mark, so we weren't as worried about trying to stop labor again if it started. The longer the babies could stay in, the better. But we also didn't want to put unnecessary stress on Georgia's body.

"Fuck," she cried out, gripping the side of the bed as her face contorted in pain.

"Go get the nurse," I instructed Dex as I ran over to the monitor that was hooked up to her and monitoring the babies. "This is a big contraction, baby. Try to breathe through it." I rubbed her back and hated that she was in so much pain.

The door opened and a nurse rushed in with Dex following behind her.

"You're doing great," the nurse said as I moved out of the way so she could see the monitor. "Nice, deep breaths if you can. This one is almost over."

Georgia continued to grip the side of the bed as she waited for it to stop while the nurse used the phone they always kept on them and asked someone to send Georgia's doctor in.

As soon as the contraction ended, Georgia fell back against the pillow and let out a heavy breath.

"That was the strongest one I've had," she said to the nurse who was studying her vitals, and then looked at Georgia.

"Yeah, they get like that. Doctor Greene is on her way to check you. We'll know more soon," she said with a soft smile.

Just then, the door opened, and the doctor smiled at all of us, already used to both Dex and me being constantly at Georgia's bedside.

"Good morning," she greeted as she stood beside the bed and looked at the monitors. "You've been having contractions for the past hour or so, but it looks like they're getting more intense and more frequent."

"I honestly didn't feel much before that one. I was sleeping pretty good, which seems weird that I could sleep through them," Georgia said.

"Some contractions are very mild, especially in early labor," Doctor Greene replied.

"I'm in labor?"

The look on Georgia's face was priceless, as if this was news she hadn't expected.

"You are. I would like to check your cervix to see how things are progressing, but yes, you are in labor. Congratulations on making it to the thirty-five-week mark."

"It seems like it's taken forever to get here," Georgia admitted. "I thought I was going to have to live here."

Everyone laughed, but I couldn't help the overwhelming excitement I felt about getting to meet our babies soon.

"If you two want to go grab a cup of coffee or something, I'm going to check Georgia real quick. We'll have a good idea of how far she's dilated and make a plan from there."

I nodded and took a deep breath as Dex and I stepped out into the hallway and closed the door behind us to give her some privacy.

"Are you okay?" Dex asked, clapping a hand on my shoulder.

"Yeah. Fuck." I blew out a breath and looked at him, knowing how frazzled I must have seemed. "We're having babies today."

"It appears that way," he replied with a laugh. "Everything is going to be fine. Georgia and the babies are going to do great."

"Why am I so nervous? I fucking want these babies more than anything, and now suddenly I feel like I'm going to crawl out of my skin and fuck everything up because they're coming."

"I think it's normal for dads to feel like that before their baby is born."

"You're not freaking out," I objected, looking him up and down and judging how calm and collected he was.

"I already had my freak out, remember? Now I'm good and here to take care of both of you. We've got this."

Just then, the door opened and Doctor Greene stepped out.

"Georgia is dilated to five centimeters, so we're going to keep a close eye on her and monitor her contractions. Labor can take hours or minutes. It's always hard to tell. What I recommend is getting anything you need now, so you can be there to support her like both of you have been."

"Thank you," I said, nodding my head in agreement.

"I will be back in a little bit. The nurses will be monitoring her on the screens at their desks and checking in with her frequently. If you need anything, just press the call button or come grab one of us."

"Will do. Thank you," Dex answered before we went back inside the room and found Georgia resting in bed.

"The babies are coming," she said, her voice filled with a mixture of happiness and fear as it broke at the last second, and a tear slid down her face.

"They are," I replied, sitting beside her and holding her hand. "How are you feeling?"

"Scared," she admitted, trying to stop the tears but failing when Dex sat on the other side and held her other hand. "What if I can't do this?"

"You can, baby. We're here to help you—all of us. You have a great doctor, and she has a fantastic team. We've got this," I assured her, feeling stronger than I had a few minutes ago.

"It's two babies. Like two whole humans that I have to get out of my body," she murmured, looking straight ahead instead of at us.

"You are so strong, Georgia," Dex said, pulling her attention to him. "You carried these babies for thirty-five weeks and kept them healthy. You can do this. I know you can. We're here for you every step of the way."

She took a deep breath and blew it out as she nodded. Then another contraction started, and my attention was no longer on me or how I felt about everything. It was on my wife and making sure she was okay as she brought our babies into the world.

Forty-Seven

Georgia

"Push," Doctor Greene said as she sat on the chair between my legs and held the baby's head as I bore down and pushed as hard as I could. "That's it. Another push, Georgia. Harder and longer this time."

I took a deep breath and then closed my eyes and pushed as hard as I could as I felt the baby slide out, feeling instant relief when the pressure was no longer there. I leaned back against the bed, which was raised so I didn't have to hold myself up more than needed while pushing.

The silence was deafening as I waited to hear the baby cry. I watched as Doctor Greene wiped its face and suctioned its nose, then suddenly it started to cry, the most beautiful sound I'd ever heard.

"Congratulations," Doctor Greene said, showing me the baby before they swaddled it. "It's a boy!"

We had purposely not found out the gender of the babies because I wanted it to be a surprise. Even though we had so many other surprises—like the pregnancy in general, and not knowing who the father was— but this one felt like a fun surprise that we could celebrate when the babies got there.

"Oh my gosh! A boy!" I squealed, looking at Dex and Alex as they beamed with pride and happiness.

Doctor Greene passed the baby to one of the nurses, who then took it to the corner of the room where they had everything set up to get his measurements and vitals. Then she looked at the monitor and smiled at me.

"Another contraction is starting soon. We're going to go straight back into pushing, okay?"

I nodded, feeling more confident that I could do this even though I was more tired than I had expected.

Before I could say anything, the contraction started, and the familiar feeling of pain hit me again. I felt Dex and Alex's hands on me as they tried to soothe me, but the only thing that would take the edge off was to deliver the baby.

"Great job. Keep pushing," Doctor Greene said.

I did as she asked and then felt the relief as it ended. I took a deep breath and let my head rest for a few before the next contraction started. She had warned that the second baby typically came pretty fast after the first baby, so I was hoping she was right.

We went through a few more contractions, and I was starting to lose hope when she grinned at me and said she saw the head. That was my motivation to keep pushing, regardless of how tired I felt.

"Baby's head is out. Keep pushing, Georgia."

I grunted and bore down, giving it everything I had as I felt the second baby slide out. My body was weak and exhausted as I laid there, watching as she suctioned its nose as well. Then the sweet sound of crying filled the room, promising me that my babies were okay.

"Congratulations," Doctor Greene said with a warm smile as she turned the baby to face me. "It's a girl!"

I clasped my hand over my mouth and shook my head in disbelief as happy tears made their way down my face.

Forty-Eight

Georgia

It was a wonderful sight to see Dex and Alex sitting on the couch in the postpartum room, each of them holding a baby while I ate some lunch. My body was still exhausted, but the carbs were helping me get some energy as I stuffed a few fries into my mouth and grinned at how cute my guys looked.

There was constant traffic in my room with nurses coming to check on me, while others helped me with breastfeeding and getting the babies to latch. It was wonderful to have the support of everyone, especially when I felt too tired to remember any of this once we were discharged. But thankfully, the guys asked a million questions, so I didn't have to worry about whether they would remember once we left.

I was finishing my sandwich when Doctor Greene came in with another woman.

"How are you feeling?" she asked, standing beside me and smiling at the guys.

"Tired. But I'm thankful those contractions are over," I joked.

"I bet. You did a great job, Georgia. I'm heading out for the day, but just wanted to come and check on you. If you need anything, just give the office a call."

"Thank you. I appreciate everything you did."

"My pleasure. Before I go, this is Heather. She's going to collect the information for the babies so we can submit the paperwork for their birth certificates," Doctor Greene explained.

The woman smiled and held her clipboard against her chest.

"Oh. Ummm," I hesitated, unsure of how to ask the question I didn't want to ask. "About that."

Doctor Greene tilted her head and waited patiently.

"I don't know what to put for the father of the babies... There's umm... We don't know who the father is because we... Umm. Yeah. So, it was consensual and we all agreed—"

Doctor Greene held her hand up and stopped me.

"It's not a problem at all. We can hold off on listing the father's name if you would like to wait until you can have a paternity test done," Doctor Greene said.

I blew out a breath of relief.

"Do you know how we go about requesting one?" Alex asked.

"You can order one through an accredited lab, or you can do an at-home one. The at-home ones are pretty reliable and a lot less expensive than going through the lab. But that is up to you guys and what your preference is. If you need it for legal purposes, you will need to go through a lab."

"No, we don't need it for legal purposes," I explained as I smiled at the guys. "We just want to know for ourselves."

"I would try the at home one, but if you have any questions, you know where to find me." Doctor Greene grinned and then waved as she left.

The guys were busy with the babies while I completed the portions of the paperwork that I could. I didn't want to just arbitrarily put Alex's information on the birth certificates just because he was my husband. That wasn't fair to Dex since there was an equal chance the babies could be his.

I rested for a bit while the guys swapped babies, but it only lasted a little while before they both woke up hungry and showed us just how loud they could cry.

Forty-Nine

Alex

"I don't understand," I said as we sat in Doctor Greene's office and listened to her explain the results of the paternity test.

We started with the at home tests, but when we found that both Dex and I were the father, we figured they were faulty and decided to go through a lab.

"Heteropaternal superfecundation is a rare phenomenon where twins have different biological fathers," Doctor Greene explained as she placed her hands on the papers in front of her and looked at the three of us while the babies slept soundly in their double stroller.

"The twins seriously have different fathers?" Georgia questioned in disbelief.

"Yes. Given the information you provided about when you conceived, it definitely explains it. Having missed your birth control pills and having sperm from two separate individuals can allow two eggs to be fertilized by different sperm."

"This is unbelievable," Dex said, slouching in the chair as he ran a hand over the scruff on his jaw. We were all balancing the late nights and little sleep, which showed with the amount of scruff we both currently had.

"According to the results, Alex is the father of Daisy, and Dex is the father of Ben." Doctor Greene slid the paperwork back over to us as I processed the news. While we all knew that both of the babies were ours and that it didn't matter who the actual father was, there was something soothing about knowing.

"Wow," Georgia said, her eyes wide as she looked at the paperwork. "That is unbelievable. Leave it to you guys to be in competition with who could knock me up first, that you had to do it at the same time."

Everyone laughed, which helped lighten the mood.

We thanked Doctor Greene for her time and headed home, which was my new favorite place to be.

Having Georgia in my life was the greatest joy I thought I could ever know. Adding in my best friend and our children was the best gift I had ever been given, and I was going to spend all of my days being thankful for it.

Fifty
Georgia
Christmas Day

"Do you think they like their presents?" Dex asked, watching the babies as they sat in Alex's lap on the floor, playing with the fabric books Dex had picked for them.

"They love them," I said with a smile, loving how much he cared about our babies.

It had been a long few months as we all tried to navigate things as new parents, but having both of them home with me had been wonderful. I loved that they didn't have to rush off anywhere and that we were able to lean on each other for support. While I was used to being home all the time since I didn't work, it was incredibly relieving to see them so carefree and without the stress of worrying about work.

After finding out that they had each fathered one of the twins, we laughed about how fate sealed our future together. While Dex and I would never be able to legally get married, we wore rings that we bought for each other to symbolize our love and devotion to one another.

We'd spent time as a family decorating for Christmas right after Thanksgiving, but I couldn't help but think back to a year ago when everything changed between us. While it was completely unexpected, I wouldn't change what happened at the cabin for anything in the world. Not only did it bring Dex and me closer, but it also gave us our beautiful children, who filled all of our lives with so much joy.

I tucked my feet under me on the couch and grinned as the babies started squealing as Dex got down on the carpet in front of them and played peek a boo. It felt like they were changing so quickly, but I loved watching them grow and couldn't wait to see what their personalities were as they got older.

I sat there and watched the two men whom I loved more than my heart could handle play with the two tiny humans we created that I loved more than anything in the world.

"Keep looking at me like that and I'll knock you up again," Alex warned, lifting his eyes to meet mine.

"Is that a threat or a promise?" I teased, lifting my coffee mug to my lips and taking a sip.

"Both," Dex answered for him. "In case you haven't noticed, we're quite obsessed with you, and both of us can't wait to have more babies with you."

"We already have our hands full with twins," I reminded both of them with raised eyebrows.

"Eh, they're not that hard. I could easily take on a few more," Dex said with a lopsided grin.

"Me too," Alex agreed.

"You guys can't be serious," I replied with a laugh. "You want more children already?"

"Not right this moment," Alex said softly. "But maybe we can start trying again in a year or two."

"I agree. I want to enjoy our time with the babies and soak up every second we have with them, but I would also love to have more babies with you, Georgia."

"I guess it would be different if we actually *planned* it this time," I teased. "Not like last time, though I'm not complaining."

"We could always go back up to the cabin for a round two," Alex offered as he wiggled his eyebrows.

"I don't think things will quite be the same when we go up there with the twins." I laughed. "Plus, I don't know how well we would do if we got stranded up there and didn't have all of their favorite toys. They would probably be really disappointed."

"Yeah, that was a wild trip up there," Dex agreed.

"Shit. It was a wild winter in general," Alex added. "Between getting stuck in a blizzard for weeks and knocking Georgia up, it was pretty wild. But I would do it all over again, hands down."

"It was pretty wild, but I'm thankful for everything that happened," I said softly as I smiled at my family. "Getting stuck in that cabin brought me everything I could ever want or need."

****

Looking for more holiday romance? Be sure to check out my Sugarplum Falls series!

Want to hang out and chat about books? Find me in my reader group! I would love to have you!

https://www.facebook.com/groups/2945710968775398/

282

Other Books By Samantha Baca

<u>Romantic Suspense</u>

The Haven Brook Series

(small-town romantic suspense)

'Til Death Do Us Part (Haven Brook Book 1) | The Cradle Will Fall (Haven Brook Book 2)

The Ties That Bind (Haven Brook Book 3) | A Very Haven Christmas (Haven Brook Book 4- Novella) | Three Strikes, You're Gone (Haven Brook Book 5)

The Dark Shadows Trilogy

(romantic suspense)

Five Steps Ahead (Dark Shadows Book 1) |Ten Seconds Too Late (Dark Shadows Book 2) | Against The Clock (Dark Shadows Book 3)

Broken (Standalone)

Romantic Comedy

Beaumont Creek Series

Just One Time | Second Chances | Third Time's The Charm | Four-ever Single | Fifth Wheel

Whiskey Mountain Series

Something To Talk About | Something To Think About | Something To Believe In | Something To Live For

Holiday Novellas

Sugarplum Falls Series

(Holiday Novellas- can be read as standalone)

Blame It On The Mistletoe | Blame It On The Eggnog | Blame It On The Candy Canes
Blame It On The Blizzard | Blame It On The Reindeer | Blame It On The Carols | Blame It On The Lattes | Blame It On The Secret Santa | Blame It On The Holidays: A collection of bonus epilogues

The Stone Creek Series

(small town novellas)

Chocolate Covered Mistletoe (Stone Creek Book 1) | Candy Coated Promises (Stone Creek Book 2) | Pumpkin Spiced Possibilities (Stone Creek Book 3)

Wild Winter

Standalone Holiday Novellas

Snow Place To Go | A Very Merry Kissmas | A Christmas
Wish | Holiday Hijinks

Standalone Holiday Full Length

Wild Winter

<u>Standalone Books</u>

One Last Wish | Finding Love In Apartment 2C (novella)
| Breaking All The Rules (Previously published as: Cocky
Counsel: A Hero Club Novel)_All Is Fair In Food And War
(novella)

Acknowledgments

How is it possible that I have written 39 books? That sounds so wild and unbelievable, especially when I went into this thinking that I would only write one and then I would be done. I am so grateful for the love and support that I have received along the way, as well as the encouragement to keep going.

I couldn't do any of this without my alpha and beta readers. A huge, giant thank you to Azucena, Claire, Tamara, Valerie, and Malissa for guiding me through the early stages of this book and helping me to get everything right. I appreciate you ladies so much! I'd also be lost without the help of my beta readers who let me know what we might have missed along the way and help polish each book to make it the best it can be! Your help is always so incredibly valuable and I will never take it for granted! Thank you, Amanda, Reina, Jackie, and Karrie for all you do!

I also couldn't do any of this without the constant love and support of my family. They believe in me when I find myself doubting that I can do this, and they continue to be my biggest supporters.

To my readers—thank you for being you and for giving my books a chance! I know there are so many other options to choose from so thank you for picking me!

My girls, you are getting older but no, you still cannot read my books. We'll talk when you're adults and see if you still want to read my books! But I will say that your support of me and my books warms my heart every single day. Thank you for loving me so unconditionally and for always telling everyone that your mommy is an author. I love you both so much!

And last, but not least, to the biggest Dick I've ever met. Thank you for being you. You are amazing and I'm so lucky to have you as my partner in cri—life. I mean *life*. We can talk about the other thing later when no one is reading this… But seriously, thank you for busting your butt every single day to provide for your family. Your efforts and sacrifices do not go unnoticed or unappreciated. I hope you always know how much you mean to me. I love you!

About the Author

Samantha lives in the southwest with her husband and two children, where she enjoys writing, drinking iced coffee, and watching the greatest show of all time—Friends. With over 30 books published, Samantha enjoys writing across several different genres, from steamy romantic suspense to laugh-out-loud spicy romantic comedies. She also has a sweet spot for holiday stories, so grab a blanket and get ready to binge some of the sweetest—yet spicy—holiday romance your heart can handle!

Samantha loves connecting with her readers, so here's a list of where you can find her:

Facebook Reader Group:

https://www.facebook.com/groups/2945710968775398/

Facebook:

https://www.facebook.com/AuthorSamanthaBaca

Instagram:

https://instagram.com/author_samantha_baca

Webpage:

www.samanthabaca.com

Goodreads:

http://www.goodreads.com/authorsamanthabaca

Books2Read:

https://books2read.com/ap/RQAYK9/Samantha-Baca

www.ingramcontent.com/pod-product-compliance
Lightning Source LLC
Chambersburg PA
CBHW061221310726
48971CB00007B/1895